CW01431315

A Stroke of The Pen

Francis Brown

authorHOUSE®

AuthorHouse™ UK Ltd.
500 Avebury Boulevard
Central Milton Keynes, MK9 2BE
www.authorhouse.co.uk
Phone: 08001974150

© 2010 Francis Brown. All rights reserved.

No part of this book may be reproduced, stored in a retrieval system, or transmitted by any means without the written permission of the author.

First published by AuthorHouse   6/15/2010

ISBN: 978-1-4520-0809-7 (sc)

This book is printed on acid-free paper.

To my wife Barbara.

Foreword

"The author Francis Brown possesses the writing skills to keep any writer totally absorbed in his varied and enthralling short stories. In true Hitchcock style he conjures up a surprise to keep you guessing to the very last line."

Alan N. V. Williams F.B.I.I.

Introduction.

I was born in County Down, Northern Ireland towards the end of the Second World War. A product, or perhaps a by-product, of Regent House Grammar School, I went on to do an engineering apprenticeship. In 1990 I moved to live in Plymouth in Devon and decided to have a complete career change, going into Care Work in nursing and residential homes, and E.M.I. units. This was followed by a move to York in 1992, where I continued in Care Work gaining a City and Guilds Diploma in Community Care Practice. For the last few years I have been involved in Community Services transporting elderly, disabled people and adults with learning difficulties to and from day services in the York Area.

Over a few years I have written some short stories and poems, mainly for my own amusement. Following a slight stroke in 2007 and now retired, I decided it was a good time to progress with my writing.

As a member of the York Writers group, I made the decision to put my short stories and poems together in this book with the view that all proceeds be donated to The Stroke Association charity, my way of saying thank you for the care I received.

Francis Brown

Acknowledgements

Thanks to my wife Barbara for the word processing, proof reading, and the putting together of these bits and pieces into some intelligible order.

My thanks also to Alan Williams of the Sun Inn, Acomb, for proof reading, and for his support and encouragement.

Thanks to all of the staff at the Acute Stroke Unit at York District Hospital for the care received in July 2007.

Contents

'Taps' Magee

The die was cast. My wife Barbara and I had finally made our long awaited decision. We had sold our pub and restaurant in Plymouth and were thinking of moving to live somewhere in Lancashire, where we hoped to buy a house or a cottage. We had chosen this particular area for the simple reason we had fallen in love with Lancashire and the Fylde coast. The intention was to retire from being pub landlords and enjoy a well earned rest from seven day weeks and long working days.

Unfortunately for us we discovered the Dog and Parrot Inn, a beautiful little hostelry situated half way down the main street in Ableton. Ableton, with a population of about three thousand, was situated high up on the fells overlooking the M6 motorway, placing it mid way between Lancaster and Preston. We had been driving through the village on a particularly pleasant spring day, when we decided to stop for a spot of lunch. We were on our way back to Blackpool where we were staying for a few days. Barbara parked the car in the sizeable parking area situated behind the main buildings, which we entered from the main street by driving under a large, stone built archway. Certainly there was more to the Dog and Parrot Inn than was immediately obvious from its frontage.

We were impressed from the moment we entered. The whole place had a buzz and vitality about it. It was warm and welcoming

1

and although it was probably past the peak of the lunchtime rush, it was still busy. We bought a drink at the well stocked bar and were served by a pleasant and efficient barman. When we asked if we were too late for lunch, he assured us that there was absolutely no problem and took our order. We found a table by the window and a young waitress came and set the table with shining cutlery and fresh cotton napkins, making sure that the condiments were present and filled up, whilst all the time smiling pleasantly. The same young lady returned a few minutes later with our meal, which was beautifully prepared and presented. She wished us 'bon appétit' and left us to enjoy it.

A little later, as we were finishing off, a gentleman who introduced himself as John Hawkins the owner of the establishment came over to ask if we had enjoyed our meal. We, of course, replied enthusiastically in the affirmative. Barbara explained that, like himself, we had aimed for similar high standards in our own business in Plymouth. He immediately became very interested and we told him that we had just sold it and, we were hoping to find a property somewhere local to buy, as we liked the area so much. He asked us if he could join us at our table and he sat with us as we had our coffee. He sent off for another pot as we chatted about the ins and outs of catering for the general public, and the importance of finding and keeping good staff. Then he quite casually told us that he had put the business on the market the previous day, as a going concern. He had been very reluctant to do this as he and his wife had built up the business over twenty years, but she was now quite poorly. Their daughter, who lived in New Zealand, had finally coaxed them to go and live with her. John explained that the business, along with his wife and family, had been his life. He had now chosen to give up working in order to spend more time with his wife.

Barbara caught my eye across the table, the same thought had occurred to both of us. John caught the look and enquired if we would be interested. Well, some things are meant to happen, but whilst we had been looking for a break from work, here was a chance to do the things that we were good at, in the surroundings where we wanted to be. However, we decided to go away and think it over and come back to him in a few days. We exchanged phone numbers and John walked us out to our car. Just before we drove off he told us that he would like the Dog and Parrot to go to someone who would continue to provide the high standards of service that the clientele had become used to. I think he was saying to any prospective buyers that they would have to guarantee that, or forget about a deal! We fully understood that, as we had virtually done the same thing when we sold our business in Plymouth. We left, assuring him of our best intentions, and promised to contact him in a few days.

To be honest we talked about little else in the next three days. We were completely taken by the place. Its position was for us, ideal. The staff were competent and professional, so we followed up our interest. We contacted the estate agent who was handling the sale and found that the price, whilst high, was not exorbitant, and well within our budget. I rang Mr Hawkins expressing our interest, and he invited us for lunch the following Saturday.

After lunch he showed us around the buildings, some of which were over two hundred and fifty years old and well maintained. John told us some of the history of the place. Apparently the original building had been a coaching inn during the mid eighteenth century, being used as a staging post for the coach line. Spare horses were stabled there, and occasionally passengers would stay overnight and continue their journey the next day. There were originally three two storey cottages, that had housed the farriers and stable lads and their families, who tended the spare horses. These were now modernised being converted into six en suite rooms, available for customers who wished to stay at the inn. These, John assured us, were an excellent source of income all year round. Next we visited the cellars which were huge and ran underneath the main building, virtually from end to end. They appeared to be much too large for their purpose, but as the owner explained, in the past they had been used for all sorts of things. They stored grain and supplies for hard winters, and even for keeping bodies in during various epidemics, which had come upon the area in bygone days.

We then had a tour of the kitchens, and Barbara came into her own in this area. This had been her forte in our previous hostelry. We were introduced to the staff, who had all been informed of our interest in buying the going concern. They all seemed to be happy enough about that.

However there is more to buying a business than just bricks and mortar so I arranged for my accountant to examine the books, and for a surveyor to check the buildings over, all of which the owner was more than happy with.

So we arranged that when these tasks had been carried out satisfactorily, we would meet with him again to table an offer for the business. To be honest we didn't expect any problems, and there were none. In just over three weeks we were sitting around a table with John, sorting out the financial side of things. It all went incredibly smoothly. Just before we actually signed anything he said there was one thing he had to mention before the deal was finalised. We waited with some trepidation to hear what he had to say, we had thought things were going too smoothly! He surprised us totally when he explained that the Dog and Parrot Inn had in fact got its own resident ghost, poltergeist, spirit, call it what you will. We listened intently as John related a series of events such as, lights being turned on and off in the cellar, beer pumps not working when there was nothing wrong with them and the occasional sighting of a strange figure in the cellar and in the newly converted cottages. No one had ever been harmed, but one or two of the staff had been frightened enough to leave their jobs. All of the present staff were quite used to the activity of whatever or whoever it was and accepted it as part and parcel of the job.

John then related the story of a young man who had looked after the dray horses at the inn in the mid eighteen hundreds, when a local brewery owned it. This young man, according to the folklore of the time, was a veteran of the Crimean war. Apparently his name was Michael Magee, known as Taps, because of his habit of having his boot heels tipped with steel wedges. He had been a member of the 13th Light Dragoons, of the Charge of the Light Brigade fame at Balaclava. Wounded several times he had survived the Charge. Unfortunately his wounds were bad enough for him to be repatriated back to England where he eventually recovered, but was unable to stay in the army. Taps went back to Ireland, married his sweetheart Mary and, when fully recovered from his injuries, returned to England to find work. Ireland at the time was in the grip of the Great Famine. The potato crop, on which the population had depended for food, had failed again and work was difficult to find.

Michael found work as a farrier and general factotum, looking after the horses and wagons at the brewery which was on the same site as the Earl of Lancaster Inn at Ableton. His experience with horses in the army and his record at Balaclava stood him in good stead. He was soon sending money home to his beloved wife, Mary. He was a hard worker, kind and considerate to all who knew him.

After about eighteen months of working for the brewery he told his workmates that he was about to send for Mary. He had been promised one of the three cottages at the back of the Earl of Lancaster Inn, as the Dog and Parrot was then called. One day a dray wagon was being unloaded, its two large horses standing quietly, snuffling in their feed bags. A local farmer, in the village for supplies, accidentally discharged his musket. He habitually carried it on his cart in case he spotted something for the pot, and also for protection.

The dray horses, startled, reared up and bolted down the street where several of the local children were playing. Taps, seeing the danger, threw himself onto one of the horses, pulling desperately on the bridle in a gallant effort to steer the terrified animals and the heavily laden cart, away from the children. This he managed to do, but the cart struck the corner of a building, tipping the cart and its load of heavy barrels onto the road, at high speed. One of the horses was killed, and Taps was seriously injured. The local doctor was called, but unfortunately arrived too late to save him and he subsequently died of his injuries. He was twenty seven years old.

Taps stock in the area was already high with his employers, and all who knew him, but the gratitude of the residents of Ableton and the surrounding district knew no bounds. He had given his life to protect those children and everyone was keen to acknowledge that. A collection was taken and everyone from the richest to the poorest in the area contributed. His employers at the brewery donated one hundred pounds, a huge sum in those days. He was buried with full military honours, in the local churchyard. The sum of money raised by the collection, which was considerable, was sent with the deepest condolences and sympathy of all concerned, to his young widow in Ireland.

Everyone was quiet for a moment when John finished the tale. It was, he said, only his opinion, but he believed that whoever it was in the cellar, the chances were that it was Michael Magee. He was so close to being reunited with his wife when it all went tragically wrong.

Barbara and I listened with rapt attention. We had heard of many old inns and public houses being haunted and it only seemed to give them a bit of character, so at the end of the day, it did not deter us from completing the purchase of the Dog and Parrot. All of the staff were more than happy to stay on and work for us and as they were a good bunch, we were delighted to have them.

And so the old inn moved on into a new era. We had a grand opening night and introduced ourselves to the locals. Everything went extremely well. The staff excelled themselves and a most enjoyable evening was had by all, except you know who!

It was well after midnight and all the staff had gone home, except Tom the bar manager. Tom had stayed to sort out some stock in the cellar in preparation for the next day. He had been down there for about half an hour. Barbara and I were having a well earned nightcap when we suddenly heard him calling. We went to the top of the cellar steps and found that the lights had gone out. I shouted down to Tom who seemed to be in a bit of a panic. He said he could hear something or someone walking about. I checked the fuses on the main switchboard but they appeared to be in order, so I collected large torch and, leaving Barbara at the top of the stairs, I went down into the cellar. Tom met me at the bottom of the steps, so by the light of the torch we found our way to the light switch and found it to be still in the *on* position. As we stood there in torchlight I distinctly heard the sound of footsteps walking across the bluestone flagged floor. It sounded like someone who had steel heel tips on their boots or shoes. The footsteps headed off to the other end of the cellar and finally stopped. I felt the hair rise on the back of my neck, and a moment later, to my great relief, the lights came back on. Tom and I searched the cellar from end to end, but found nothing out of the ordinary.

I decided next day that I would have an electrician in to check out the wiring and fuses. I didn't want a repeat of that little scenario again. It was lucky that Tom was a level headed individual and not in the least bit fazed by the goings on. As he said, similar things had happened before and might happen again.

The electrician arrived the next morning, about an hour after I had phoned him. Luckily for me he had just had a cancellation. After a thorough check of all our electrical wiring and equipment he was unable to find any fault whatsoever, so we kept an open mind as to the cause of the problem.

Things seemed to get worse, certainly the frequency of these events increased over the next few weeks. Perhaps whoever or whatever it was, was trying to impress the new owners. Staff were becoming totally fed up of having to clear up after 'happenings', not only in the cellar but in the rest of the building as well. Water taps were turned on, barrels of ale leaked all over the cellar floor, and glasses and bottles were broken. Luckily most of these happened after staff had gone home and Barbara and I were asleep in our flat on the top floor. All the same, the mess had to be cleared up before we opened for business the next day.

Then one night I was awoken by a loud crash which could only have come from the cellar. The bedside clock showed two a.m. By this time enough was enough. I dressed quickly without waking Barbara. I stormed down the stairs to the cellar door. I went down the steps to find that a large barrel of ale had been tipped off the top of a stack and had crashed onto the stone floor, breaking off the valve and spewing ale everywhere. I was absolutely livid! Any feeling of fear or apprehension about meeting up with whatever it was, disappeared in a red mist. I decided that I was staying there until I had said my piece to whatever it was. I could see no-one in the cellar so I went over to an old armchair which was in the middle of the floor and sat down on it.

"Okay," I shouted, "Let's have a look at you, whoever you are. Are you going to be a man or do you want to play silly buggers!"

The lights went out.

The cellar was silent. I sat in the chair gripping the armrests very tightly. My anger and bravado had disappeared like snow off a dyke. I was absolutely terrified.

The silence deepened. The darkness touchable.

I don't know how long I sat there hardly daring to breathe. I became totally disorientated with nothing tangible to focus on. Barbara must still be asleep, so I was totally on my own. Or was I? I became aware of footsteps. Boots with iron tipped heels by the sound of them, coming closer, closer, and still closer. If I thought that I was frightened before, then now I was totally petrified. The footsteps stopped in front of the chair. The darkness was absolute, like black velvet. Whoever it was could see a lot better than I could.

I summoned up all my courage.

"Who are you?" I croaked.

The boots shuffled a little.

"Can you speak?" I squeaked. The only sound my ragged breathing.

"Look," I said, gathering my courage in both hands, "This cannot go on. What do you want?"

Silence.

"Right then, do you want to communicate?"

Silence.

"Okay then," I said, trying desperately to think of something to break this impasse, "knock once for yes and twice for no. Do you understand?" - It sounds laughable now, but I'd heard someone say it in a movie once.

Knock!

I almost fell out of the chair! The darkness was deeper than ever. The air in the cellar felt almost icy. I was beginning to shiver, whether from cold or fear, or a combination of both I didn't know. Right, what's my next question, I asked my addled brain.

"Are you Michael Magee?" I asked my voice about two octaves higher than usual. That was me, straight to the point as usual.

Knock.

"Known as Taps?"

Knock.

"Why do you cause all this trouble here, Taps?" I was growing in confidence a little.

Silence.

"Do you want to harm us?"

Knock Knock.

"Are you a spirit?"

Knock.

"Don't you want to be here?"

Knock Knock.

"Where do you want to be?"

Silence.

"I believe you originally came from Ireland, is that correct?"

Knock.

"Do you want to be in Ireland, then?"

Knock. Then violent knocking.

"Back to where you used to live with your wife, Mary?"

Violent knocking.

"As a spirit or ghost or whatever you are, can you not just go there on your own?"

Knock Knock.

"Why not?"

Silence.

On the one hand I was tempted to believe that everything that had happened was one great wind up. That in a minute someone would jump out and shout 'April Fool' or something similar and we would all fall about laughing. On the other hand, if all of this was real, then here was a man, a hero of his time if you like, who was finally able to communicate from beyond the grave. To make his feelings known in the hope that someone can help him to return to the land of his birth. Somehow I just knew that this was for real. Should I turn away from someone who unselfishly gave his own life, albeit a century and a half ago, to save others? I couldn't do that, but god help anyone who was taking the pee!

"Taps, you are creating all sorts of problems for me and my staff. If I try to find a way to get you back to Ireland, will you promise to stop all this activity of yours?"

KNOCK.   KNOCK.   KNOCK.

"Right," I said, I'll take that as a yes, but you must give me some time to find someone who knows about these things."

I was warming to my subject now and feeling more at ease with whoever it was that I was communicating with. At least I thought I knew who it was supposed to be.

"How long will you give me Taps? It could take some time. Knock once for each week that I can have, bearing in mind that you have been waiting for a long time."

The silence grew deeper again, and I was beginning to think that I had overplayed my hand. Then,

Knock   Knock   Knock   Knock

"Four weeks, Taps. I promise I'll find out how to work this. Now you keep your part of the bargain and I'll keep mine." God help me, I thought to myself, if I fail. There was silence for a moment and then came the sound of footsteps heading off towards the other end of the cellar. I sat absolutely still, frightened to move a muscle. Suddenly the lights came on. I was blinded by their brightness for a moment. I stood up quite shakily, trying to work the stiffness out of my joints. The chill air in the cellar had not helped either. I looked all around. I was alone.

Looking at my watch I saw that it was seven minutes past two. Less than ten minutes had elapsed since I had entered the cellar.

Next morning I told Barbara about the night before, and of my promise to help Taps Magee. Only the fact that she knows me very well or I imagine she would have thought that I was beginning to crack up.

"Where," I asked her, "do you find out how to transport a ghost, spirit, call it what you will back to its own country?"

Well, we started at the local library, reading all sorts of books on the supernatural. We had tried all sorts of so called experts, but most of them didn't have a clue or could even be really helpful in any way shape or form. We progressed to the Yellow Pages, and finished up with our local vicar.

Time was moving on and we had a little over two weeks left out of our agreed four. In total desperation I rang our local vicar, the

Reverend Thomas Berkley MA, at the Manse in our village. We were invited round for afternoon tea.

He and Mrs Berkley welcomed us into their home, and while his wife went off to put the kettle on, he listened patiently to our tale. He had been aware that the Dog and Parrot Inn had been troubled by a spirit of some sort for a long time. No one had been able to find out who it was, so in this respect at least we had made some progress. The vicar's wife returned with tea and biscuits. Whilst she poured the tea the vicar excused himself for a few minutes. He returned shortly carrying an old leather bound ledger.

"The Parish Records," he said, holding it up. He carried it over to a large desk in the corner of the room and began leafing through its pages, until he found the one that he was looking for. He called us over to look at the entry. It was dated the 28th of September 1858. It read, 'Michael Magee, veteran of Balaclava and late of the Light Brigade, mortally injured saving life and limb of other parishioners in a tragic incident. Mr Magee was twenty seven years old, a married man, and a native of Ireland, where his wife still resides in their home in County Cork. Buried with full military honours.

"So here is your ghost then, the cause of all your problems. A brave and good man it appears," the vicar added.

Barbara and I agreed, and so I told him of my frightening encounter with, and my subsequent promise to Michael Magee.

"I suppose you think that I'm making a mountain out of a molehill?" I asked. He looked me straight in the eye for a minute, and then he stood up and paced up and down the room while he ordered his thoughts.

"When I was studying for the Church, theology and so on, I looked at all things to do with life and death. I read avidly everything written, not only in the Bible, but by learned people from many religious persuasions. People who had experiences such as you have had. I never closed my mind to anything in this world. One thing that did stick in my mind, and I picked it up from many sources, was that death was not necessarily the end for everyone. People have dealt with these problems in different ways. Now tell me again exactly what he wants you to do."

"Well, first and foremost, he wants to go home to Ireland. I asked him why, as a free spirit, so to speak, he doesn't just go there. He says that he cannot do that. I thought that it would have been possible now that he doesn't have an earthly body."

The vicar thought for a moment and then said, "He is possibly right. Another thing I particularly remember from long ago is that spirits cannot cross water. They are confined within the land areas where they died. So the simple answer to the question is, no he can't do that."

"How then am I going to honour my promise to him, vicar?"

Then Barbara made a suggestion, "How would it be if we had a box of earth, I don't know what size, and get him to stay there until we get the car over on the ferry?"

"That's a good idea," said the vicar, "that might have possibilities. I vaguely remember someone telling me that they had tried doing that a long while ago but it failed to work, principally because the soil must be from the place that the deceased is going to. In other words the box would have to be filled with soil from his native land, in Michael's case, Ireland, and as close as possible to where he lived."

"Do we know where he lived?" I asked.

The Reverend Berkley consulted the Parish Records again and read out an address in County Cork in southern Ireland, and whilst I wrote this down he continued to look at the ledger. He then checked his watch and I suddenly realised that we were taking up his valuable time, and had probably overstayed our welcome. We were about to take our leave when he sent a chill up my spine by saying,

"Michael Magee died on the 28th of September, 1858. His date of birth was the 28th of September, 1831. Today is the 13th of September 2008. You have just over two weeks left of the time he's given you to get him back home. Coincidence or what? That would be the one hundred and fiftieth anniversary of his death. Perhaps that is why you have been getting all this activity?"

We left the manse in thoughtful mood, having thanked the vicar and his wife profusely for their help with our problem, and promising that we would let them know the outcome.

That night, after the staff had gone home, I went down to the cellar. I left Barbara in our flat as I wanted to bring Taps up to date with our progress, and I wasn't sure how he would react to someone else being around. I was afraid that he might not even turn up, so with the cellar lights on I went and sat in the old chair again. I had just checked my watch for the umpteenth time. It was five past midnight when the lights went out.

The temperature dropped immediately. Silence. Deep silence. Pitch black. Then I heard him approaching, his heels clicking on the stone floor. Closer, and yet closer, stopping in front of my chair. Silence. Nothing. Several minutes passed. Not a sound. I was scared!

"Are you there, Taps?" I had never before called him by his nickname.

Knock.

I began rather nervously to outline our plan, the box of soil, Irish soil, and asked him if it would work.

Knock.

Luckily I had committed his address to memory, no chance of reading it in this darkness, and asked him if it was correct.

Knock.

"Are you still holding us to our time schedule?

Knock.

"Is there a reason for that?

Knock.

"Is it to do with your birthday?"

Knock.

A thought struck me, was he married on his birthday?

Knock.

Another thing occurred to me. Was Mary's birthday the same as his?

Knock.

Now I understood the urgency behind all of this. I explained that my next problem was to get a container of soil from the Cork area to the Dog and Parrot, but that I would get that organised as soon as possible. I lapsed into silence again in the darkness, not knowing what to say, and then I heard his footsteps walk around the back of my chair. I tensed up not knowing what was going to happen next.

I felt two hands, fingers spread and ice cold, on the top of my head. I gave a start, absolutely terrified, as the ghostly hands held me all too easily in the chair. I don't think that I passed out, but I certainly began to dream.

A far off land. I am on a horse, a cavalry horse, hundreds of mounted cavalry horses. My sabre is drawn. Suddenly we are charging. Gun smoke, explosions, the crackle of musket fire. Men shouting and cursing as they hack and slash at each other with sabre and bayonet. Injured horses and men screaming and dying, falling and being trampled underfoot by those following behind. Pain from my right side, but my faithful stallion races on, oblivious to the carnage around us. We are leading the charge, but only because all before us have fallen. The enemy cannon fire another massive volley of shot at point blank range, we are almost amongst them. The cannon smoke is choking us. Our lungs are bursting. My faithful steed is gasping with the effort of the never ending charge. Agony in my right shoulder, my horse, my friend, dies under me and we crash to the ground, kicked and trampled by those following behind. Darkness.

I am on a ship back to England, badly wounded, but expected to live, otherwise I would have been left to die in the field hospital. I recover, then back to my lovely Mary in Ireland. We got wed on our birthdays. She was so beautiful. We have a little money from the army, a pittance. Famine is everywhere. Mary has relatives who look after us. I have to get work back in England. Promise to send money. Get job in a brewery. Work with horses, which I'm good at. Get promoted, offered house with job, about to send for my beloved.

Gunshot. Horses bolt, children in the street. Catch reins of horses, must get them away from the children. Crash, pain, agony, worse than the war. Peaceful oblivion.

I wake up sweating, the lights are on again and I was alone.

I wept. Wept for Michael Taps Magee and his lovely Mary, and determined now, no matter what it takes, to get him home.

I related all of this to Barbara next morning over breakfast. We had only one real obstacle now to overcome, that being the appropriation of a small amount of soil from Michael's homeland. Short of actually going there and getting a bag or two of the stuff, I couldn't think of any other way to do it.

Then as usual, Barbara came up with a solution.

"Do you remember Bill Warnock from down Plymouth way?" she asked.

"Yes of course I do," I replied. "What of him?"

"What did he do for a living?"

"He ran his own transport company. I haven't seen him since we moved up here."

"Where did his trucks deliver to?" Barbara asked.

"All over the country and including Ireland," I said, and as I spoke I realised what Barbara was getting at. "Right, you think that Bill could get one of his drivers to pick up some soil from the Cork area, provided that he has one over there?"

"Yes. Why not? He'd do that for you. He owes you a few favours."

"You're right, love. It's worth a try. Have we still got his telephone number?"

"Yes. I'll go and find it," and off Barbara went.

Ten minutes later I was on the phone to Bill. He was surprised and delighted to hear from us. I brought him up to date about our move to Lancashire and the subsequent purchase of the Dog and Parrot Inn.

"Well, that is a surprise. I thought that you were finished with the pub trade and both of you were going to take things easy and live on your money."

"So did we," I said, "but the fates conspired against us, and here we are in a lovely part of the country, and doing a job that we love."

Bill told me that his own business was doing well, and that he was very busy at present.

"Can I ask you a favour, Bill? I hate to ask but I'm desperate, and I don't know of anyone else who could help."

"Ask away my friend. If I can help I will. I owe you a few favours anyway. What can I do for you?"

I told him about the soil. There was silence for a few seconds, then Bill asked,

"Are you serious?"

"Yes, but I can't tell you about it at the moment, I promise that I will when we next meet."

"OK, that's good enough for me. Where do you need this soil to come from?"

"As close to the village of Kildowney in County Cork as you can get, I reckon about fifty kilos should be enough." I replied.

"How soon do you need it?"

"Inside the next ten days, Bill."

"Right, hang on while I consult the oracle."

I could hear the sound of computer keys being punched.

"Right! I've got a truck picking up a container at Cork docks on the 19th of September, driving up to Dublin and over on the ferry to Holyhead on the twenty first. I could get him to do a slight detour to this Kildowney place. It's not much out of his way, and he can get this soil for you. How would that do? Mind you, you'll have to buy him a pint or six," said Bill, laughing.

"Sounds good to me, Bill. Many thanks."

"Now," he continued, "how do I get it to you? Hang on a sec." Computer keys again. "We have a depot in Bolton these days, so if we can get the stuff there, we have a delivery to Lancaster on the 25th of September. He can deliver to you on his way there, OK?"

"So it would be with me on the 25th, that would be excellent, Bill. Barbara and I can't thank you enough."

"My pleasure," Bill said. If there are any problems, and I don't expect any, I'll keep you informed," and wishing us both well, he hung up.

"Right," remarked Barbara, "that's sorted out."

19

"Great idea of yours. Now let's get some work done. I'll break the news to Michael later. Why don't you come down with me this time?"

"We'll see!" was her reply, and off we went back to work. We still had an Inn to run.

From the time that I had promised Michael that I would get him back home, all the strange activity had stopped, and life had returned to normal at the Dog and Parrot, much to the relief of the staff and ourselves. I kept them, as well as Michael, up to date with developments, and asked them not to talk too much outside the establishment about our problems. To give them their due, they had obliged. They were still interested though, in how things were going, as the time for Michael's departure approached. A feeling of excitement hung over the Inn.

Barbara and I were finalising our plans and making sure there would be no last minute glitches. We needed to be at Kildowney on the twenty eighth of September. The soil would arrive on the 25th. We hoped to set off in the morning of the 27th at the latest, giving us a little bit of leeway in the event of something untoward cropping up.

I decided to have a wooden box made by a local tradesman, to fit the available luggage space. I settled for a box three feet, by two feet, by twelve inches deep. This would fit neatly across the back of the car and would hold most of the soil. The box, it was promised, would be delivered by the morning of the 25th. Everything was timed to perfection, now all we could do was wait.

As usual when you work to a tight schedule, sod's law states that something will foul up the works, and so it was. We had the box, we had Michael, but the soil was delayed. We got a call from Bill, apologising profusely, telling us that the truck on the way to Lancaster had broken down on the M6 near Preston. It would now be the 27th before he could deliver. They would, he said, move heaven and earth, (excuse the pun) to get it to us on time.

They did, as well, arriving outside the Dog and Parrott at eleven forty five a.m. on the 27th. We were now against the clock and under pressure. Barbara and I decided to try to get some sleep and set off that evening. We didn't want to be dozing off at the wheel. We would still be able to arrive at Kildowney at some time on the 28th as promised. I had the car checked over and fuelled up, I didn't want any more delays. It was just after 7pm that evening when Tom the barman, and I carried the box, now filled with soil, down to the cellar to collect our passenger.

I asked Taps to get himself into the box of soil, not that I would have known whether he was there or not, and Tom and I carried it, and him, from the cellar to the back of the Volvo estate. I asked him if he was alright and got the customary single knock, meaning yes, and closed the boot lid. I had already put an overnight bag in the car and as Barbara climbed into the passenger seat, Tom locked the premises up from the inside and turned the lights off. I fired up the big engine and just after midnight we were off.

At this time of the morning Ableton was deserted, everyone was in bed, or at least indoors. I headed towards the M6 driving as fast as I could on the pitch black country roads, eventually joining the motorway at junction 32. Now I was able to make better progress. The big Volvo cruised quite happily at three figures, on the almost deserted motorway, and eventually we turned off onto the M56 and onto the A55 at junction 34, still light with traffic.

We had a quick comfort break once over the Menai Bridge and pushed on with the last leg of the journey to the Dublin ferry at the port of Holyhead. Dawn was breaking as we turned into the ferry terminal and headed for the booking office.

We were in luck. The Ferry was sailing at 09.15 and there was room for us. I purchased an open ended return ticket for the Volvo and two people, not three as I at first mistakenly asked the clerk for. (He looked at me askance, as much to say don't you know how many passengers you have in your vehicle?) We then joined the queue of cars and other vehicles waiting to board.

I explained to Taps what was going to happen, and told him that Barbara and I would not be allowed to stay in the car during the crossing, so that he would be on his own for about four hours. I asked him if he understood and he gave his usual one knock on the bodywork of the car boot. When he next saw daylight, I told him, he would be back home in Ireland.

Once parked up on the car deck, we locked up the car and went up to the passenger lounge. Our first priority was to get something to eat and drink, and secondly to try to get some sleep. We were tucking into a superb fry up before the ferry had even sailed, and within fifteen minutes of clearing the harbour were curled up fast asleep on the comfortable lounge chairs.

We were woken, what seemed like minutes later, by the call for drivers and passengers to return to their vehicles in preparation for disembarking at Dun Laoghaire.

Taps was back in his homeland.

Much refreshed by our sleep, we made good progress once we cleared the harbour complex. We stopped at a petrol station to fuel up, and bought sandwiches, cold drinks and a large scale tourist map of Ireland, then headed for Portlaoise on the M7. Taps was beginning to make a bit of a noise. I asked him if he was looking out of the window, the answer was in the affirmative. Barbara was driving now, and we were pressing on using the main roads. It was now three thirty in the afternoon and we had about five hours of daylight left. I wanted to have him delivered before darkness fell and I knew that whilst we could probably get quite close to the village of Kildowney in the Boggeragh Mountains, finding a cottage that may or may not be still standing was something else again.

The nearer we got to our destination the better the weather became. Clouds began to break up and the sun shone brightly. For the first time I began to feel positive about the outcome of our mission.

Eventually we passed through Mallow and entered the narrower roads towards Kildowney, which luckily we found signposted. We climbed slowly, if steadily upwards, twisting and turning in the rays of the setting sun. Then there was Kildowney, a main street consisting of twenty or so houses, a pub, two shops and little else.

"Have we arrived?" I asked Taps. The answer was two knocks.

"Straight on?" I asked. One knock was the reply.

We moved steadily onwards and upwards. The sun had disappeared for now and we were driving along a track a little wider than the Volvo. It was bordered on both sides by pine trees. On we went with nothing heard from Taps. I was beginning to think that perhaps he had forgotten where we were going, and then we were unexpectedly in a clearing. On both sides of the road we could see the remains of several buildings, most of which were covered in brambles. Barbara slowed the car and again I asked him if we had arrived. The answer again was a resounding no!

I was beginning to despair when we turned the next corner and found that the land fell away to the right, presenting the most amazing view of the Irish countryside for many, many miles. A vista now bathed in the late evening sunshine. At the same time Taps began banging noisily in the back and I then realised that on our left hand side was the ruin of what was a stone built cottage, its roof fallen in, the front door askew and half rotted away, and the windows long without glass. I didn't have to ask Taps this time if we had arrived! I glanced at my watch and found that it was eight fifteen. Barbara stopped the car, got out, and went round the back to open up the tail gate. I lifted out the box with the soil in and placed it on the ground. I felt him pat my shoulder. Not knowing what else to do I got back into the car. Barbara switched off the engine and we sat there in silence for a moment. Then suddenly, as if on cue, the evening sun shone directly on the old cottage and as if by magic it was totally transformed. The roof was neatly thatched, the walls whitewashed and the windows sparkled in the sunlight. The front garden was neat and tidy, with beautiful rose bushes blooming around the door, the garden gate was open. I looked across at Barbara and saw by the rapturous expression on her face that she was seeing exactly what I was seeing. We were totally unprepared for what happened next.

As we sat mesmerised and enthralled. I heard a sound, one that I had come to know very well over the past year. The sound of a certain cavalryman's boots, boots that had iron shod heels. They were approaching from behind the car, their owner marching briskly. Barbara and I sat absolutely still frightened to even blink, in case we spoiled the moment. The footsteps approached the car on the passenger side, where I sat looking straight ahead, until I could see him out of the corner of my eye as he passed by. Barbara and I could both see him by this time. A soldier, a Hussar to be precise, almost six feet tall, but looking taller wearing his Busby with the cloth bag hung from the side, obviously his dress uniform. Absolutely immaculate! Handsome in his short black jacket with the heavy gold braid on the breast, dark coloured trousers with yellow stripe, highly polished riding boots, he was a sight to behold.

He marched past the car apparently without seeing it, to the now repaired garden gate, his boots tapping on the stony path. He turned to face the little cottage. Barbara and I both heard him call 'Mary' quite loudly. A few seconds later the front door opened and a pretty young woman appeared. She was in her mid twenties, with golden, shoulder length hair and wearing a long pale blue dress and a snow white apron. She stood for a moment as if unsure as to who the soldier was, then as he doffed his Busby she quickly recognised him. She gave a cry of sheer joy and raced down the path, throwing herself at him, tears streaming down her lovely face. Taps was almost bowled over by her welcome and he lifted her off the ground and whirled her around and around, tears streaming down his own face as he kissed her again and again.

"You've come back to me Michael, I never thought that we would be together again, my darling. It's been so long." Taps hugged her long and hard.

"We're together again now my darling Mary, and never again will we be parted by anything or anyone."

They walked up the path to the front door of the beautiful little cottage wrapped up in each other's arms. The last rays of the evening sunshine lighting up the scene like something from a film set. They went inside, the door closing gently.

As if on cue the sun went in, and the little cottage that a moment ago had appeared idyllic, had once again returned to its totally run down state, leaving us for a moment wondering if we had been dreaming. We knew we had not. We shed a few tears ourselves, mostly out of happiness for Taps and Mary, also knowing what it would be like for us to be parted, as they had been. We were proud that we had done what we had. The end result was well worth the effort, even if we had nothing to show for it, except perhaps a pub with no resident ghost.

Now it was time to go home. I climbed out of the car and walked round the back to check if the hatch was shut properly and kicked something on the ground. Bending down to see what it was, I found that it was the box of soil that Taps had travelled in. I was about to put it over by the verge when I noticed something odd about it. I called for Barbara to bring the torch from the car, as the light was fading. She shone the light on the box. Impressed in the soil was the outline of a cavalry boot with iron heel tip and three words obviously drawn by a finger.

' BLESS YOU Taps'

P.S. Author's Note.

Sometime after I had put his little tale together, all fiction of course, my wife and I were on our way to the Lake District for a short holiday. We were on the M6 motorway heading north and as we approached junction 32, I had this urge to turn off and drive along the little roads climbing up towards the fells. It came to me that we were following the route that we had taken in our story, when returning Taps to his homeland. Barbara had also noticed this and we both realised that we could no more change direction than fly to the moon. It was as if we were being taken somewhere and had no control over where it might be, although a rough idea was forming in both of our minds. We drove onwards and upwards, both of us with a feeling of déjà vu, but knowing of course that there would not be a village called Ableton as the name was purely fictional. We came to a fork in the road and the car unerringly took the right road just as I caught sight of a road sign almost hidden behind tree branches. It pointed to Ableton. We arrived less than five minutes later, both of us now feeling some trepidation, like you get when you are watching a horror movie and you know just what's going to happen. As we turned into the main street we just knew that the Dog and Parrot Inn would be there, and sure enough, there it was, with its big archway into the car park. We parked up; we really didn't have any option, and went inside to have lunch. The Inn was just as we had pictured it. Everything was as I had written about it, the staff, the food, all excellent, and even a barman called Tom. As we were having our coffee a gentleman who introduced himself as John Hawkins, the owner of the establishment came over to ask if we had enjoyed our meal. We of course said that we had, and he sat down and chatted for a few minutes.

Catching Barbara's eye I asked Mr Hawkins if the Inn still had its resident ghost. He seemed a little put out at this, asking how we had known about it. I told him we had heard about it from a friend who had stayed at the Inn sometime ago. He reluctantly said that whatever it was remained in residence, all the while looking askance at Barbara and myself as though trying to remember something. He told us that two years before his wife had been very ill and he had been on the brink of selling the Dog and Parrot to a lovely couple who had been very keen on buying the business. Mr Hawkins's daughter, who lived in New Zealand, had finally convinced her parents to sell up and come and live with her and her husband. He had therefore put the business on the market, and this husband and wife who came from Plymouth, had expressed an interest in buying it. They had gone off to consider this opportunity for a few days. Then several things happened. Firstly his wife had taken a turn for the better, secondly he had received news from the police that the couple who had been interested in buying the Inn, had died in a car crash the day after their meeting with Mr Hawkins, and thirdly the Dog and Parrot Inn now had at least two resident spirits instead of one.

Harry and the Duck

Harry and I have worked together for eight years, which is almost all of his working life. I own a large sheep farm in North Yorkshire, around five hundred acres of humps and hollows, and to be honest, good staff are hard to find. When Harry came to work for me initially, he hadn't got a clue about sheep farming. Many's the time I wondered why I took him on in the first place. He was so thick it was unbelievable. He didn't know a sheep from Delaney's donkey. Anyway, I persevered with him and gradually, very, very gradually, he began to get the hang of things, just in the nick of time as I was just reaching the end of my tether with him. The problem then was that with his little bit of knowledge came the next stage of his development that all youngsters go through. Yes, it was the 'I know better than you' syndrome. I'd tell him to do something and he'd look at me like I was daft, and then do it his own way. I soon had enough of this and I had to lay it on the line to him that I was boss of this outfit and if he didn't like it he could move on. He took his time digesting this bit of information, but to give him his due, he did change. I'd give him an order, he'd still look at me like I was daft, but he would eventually do as I had told him, albeit with bad grace.

Over the years we formed a good working relationship, each of us knowing what the other was going to do. We became a very good team. Then early last spring we were bringing the flock down to the lower pastures for the lambing season. I owned an old house with a barn attached up on the moors and I kept it well stocked during this time of year, with supplies of food for Harry and I, and fodder and bedding for the ewes and lambs. I kept a petrol generator for lighting and cooking and a pile of logs and firewood to burn in an open grate in the old house. The weather could be extremely wintry on the North Yorkshire Moors and so we would stay in the old house during the lambing season, which was easier than trekking there and back every day from home.

We were moving some sheep when I noticed Harry was standing absolutely still, looking at something on the ground. I called to him but either he hadn't heard me or chose to ignore me. I made my way across to where he was standing and found an injured mallard duck lying on the ground. She looked like she had been there for a while and she was quite weak. Harry, as usual, hadn't a clue what to do so I carefully picked her up and she didn't struggle at all. A quick examination showed that she had a broken wing. Being of the opinion that all life is sacred, I decided to take her back to the house to see what could be done. It was quite late in the day and beginning to get dark. A chill easterly wind was getting up, promising sleet or even some snow before much longer. So Harry and I set off, with me carrying the injured duck as carefully as I could. It was dark when we got back so I made the little duck comfortable in a wooden box full of straw whilst I started up the generator. I then got a fire lit in the grate and soon the kitchen began to warm up and feel quite cosy. Harry seemed distraught by the plight of the duck and never took his eyes off her for a moment. I found some cloth which I tore into strips and using twigs I gently splinted the damaged wing while Harry fussed about, supervising the goings on. I managed to get a little food and water into her and put her back in the box of straw, where, completely exhausted, she slept.

Harry sat beside the box all night and woke me several times to tend to the bird. By morning I was shattered but the duck was looking a lot better. So I checked her over, left her food and water in her box and with much coaxing and cajoling eventually got Harry off to work with me. It hadn't snowed but was even colder than the previous day and I told Harry that he had probably saved the mallard's life as I was sure she would not have survived the night in the open.

We arrived back that evening to find Daphne, as we had decided to call her, much improved. She was hungry, thirsty and trying to get out of her box. Harry sat beside her while I was left to get the fire going and get us all some food. I checked her splint and after we had all eaten, set about making her a larger box from some old pieces of wood that I'd found in the barn. I made one about three feet square and a foot high, just high enough to stop her climbing out, and filled the bottom with clean straw. To this I added an old chipped enamelled dish with about four inches of water in, and a duck called Daphne. Harry who had just been sitting there taking all of this in, lay down beside the box and promptly went to sleep, as did the duck. Well, I thought, thanks for your company you two, see you in the morning, and I went off to bed. This procedure was repeated for the next two weeks with Daphne getting stronger every day. She was in and out of the water and having a great time with Harry hanging round her like a guardian angel.

She was doing so well now that I decided the time had come to see how her injuries had healed. I gently picked her up and told Harry that I was going to remove the splints. He looked at me and then at Daphne with some trepidation as I began to carefully undo the binding. It all came off quite easily and as I removed the last of it

I placed her in the bottom of her box. To my delight she immediately spread her injured wing and then flapped both wings simultaneously. As if to celebrate that all was well she splashed around in her mini swimming pool for several minutes, giving Harry a good old soaking, whilst at the same time quacking loudly.

Over the next few days she continued to get stronger. She had several short trial flights and was flying normally. I told Harry it was only a matter of time before she was off for good. Then one morning after breakfast Daphne waddled up to Harry as he sat on the front doorstep, watching her exercise her wings. She ruffled his hair with her beak, almost caressing him as he half lay there watching her. She quacked so loudly that I thought something was wrong and ran to the front door. She stretched right up to her full height and spread out both her wings, looking straight at me as she did so. She gave Harry another nuzzle, then turned and, flapping her wings faster and faster, took off. She gained height rapidly, banked round and flew low over the house before disappearing out of sight. We both knew that she had gone. Poor old Harry was distraught. Without looking at me he went quietly around the back of the house and stayed there for the rest of the day. I must confess that I was a little bit sad myself, but at the same time happy that we had helped a fellow creature when it needed us.

The lambing season was almost finished. It had been a good year all round with few problems and lots of strong, sturdy youngsters increasing our flock. The weather picked up as well with light warm winds and bright sunshine. We were almost ready to move back to the home farm and were sat outside of the old house in the early morning sunshine, finishing off a good breakfast, prepared by me of course. Harry was as usual stretched out on the long, lush grass, soaking up the heat from the sun whilst I, I must confess, was having a doze. Then into my befuddled brain came the sound of a duck quacking. In fact it sounded like several ducks. I could not believe my bleary eyes. Around the corner of the barn waddled Daphne. Harry, suddenly awake, looked like he had seen a ghost and leapt to his feet as the little duck raced to him and fussed around him affectionately. He looked absolutely gob smacked and overjoyed at the same time. Daphne turned towards the corner of the barn where she had first appeared and quacked loudly several times. Harry and I were totally unprepared for what happened next. Around the corner came a little yellow duckling, wobbling along towards its mother. This was followed by another, then another and still more until I had counted ten in all. The little flock meandered along the rough path stopping here and there to peck at some little morsel that they had spotted. In their own sweet time they moved slowly towards Harry and their mother, despite her attempts to hurry them along. Harry had by now sat down again as the little band of ducklings began to swarm around him, with Daphne in close attendance. He was very careful not to hurt any of them and they in turn were totally at ease with him. Then another surprise as around the corner of the barn, quacking loudly came a large mallard drake. Father had arrived. Daphne hurried down the path to meet him, gabbling away in duck language, and she returned with the drake to Harry and the ducklings. Harry glared at him malevolently until Daphne gave him a sharp peck as much as to say, 'Behave big boy!' Daphne and the drake wandered off a few feet and sat down in the grass soaking up the warm spring sunshine, both totally happy to leave their not so little brood in Harry's care.

I was watching Harry carefully and I noticed how his attitude towards Daphne, her family and partner had changed over the last half hour. I think that he had finally realised that she had made a new life for herself with her own kind. A life which might have ended had he not found her that fateful day. Now she had returned to say thank you and to introduce him to her new family.

He stood up tall and straight with a sort of superior look about him as he watched over the ducklings as their parents slept, accepting his new responsibilities with aplomb.

As I told him later, not many Border Collies get to be Godfather to a brood of ducklings.

My Brother's Keeper

Larry threw the Mercury into a long sliding turn off the blacktop and on to the dirt road. The old car fishtailed viciously as he mashed the gas pedal to the floor. The surface was badly rutted and the car lurched and bounced over potholes and rocks, each jolt sending waves of agony through his body. It was three fifteen in the morning, still a long way to go before sunrise, and he hurt real bad. About ten minutes later, the junction that he was looking for showed up in the feeble headlights of the old car. He almost lost control as he exited much too fast, crashing through rough scrub and small trees before skidding to a halt in a cloud of dust and gravel. He sat still for a minute, the pain in his chest now almost unbearable. He was drenched in sweat, his breathing harsh and gasping. He felt cold, freezing cold and it was all that he could do to stay awake. He killed the engine and lights, then in the darkness, slumped back in the bench seat, trying desperately to stay upright. The only sound was the ticking of the hot engine cooling down. He'd really gone and done it this time.

He slipped his hand inside the Parka jacket that he was wearing and under his shirt. He winced as he touched the hole in his chest. His hand was warm and slippery with blood as he withdrew it. He suddenly felt dizzy and he fought the nausea that threatened to overwhelm him. Why had that cop turned up when he did at two o'clock in the morning? Any other cop but that one! It was a chance in a million. A little town like Hurtsburg had little or no crime at the best of times, so why was this guy out and about at this unearthly hour when all good policemen should be getting some shuteye.

Larry closed his eyes and cried out as the pain reached new heights, helping to focus his mind on the events of the past hour and a half.

He lived on his wits, always out for the quick buck. He'd tried the lot over the six years since he had left home in a hurry, just one step ahead of a gang of his local heavies out to hurt him permanently for cutting in on their patch. He'd dabbled in drug dealing, money laundering, burglary, and even robbery as part of a gang, and never in all his twenty four years on this earth and his six years in business for himself, had anyone even remotely been hurt. That is until tonight, when that black cop turned up waving his Smith and Wesson around. Larry shivered involuntarily at the memory of events, his mind a maelstrom of thoughts.

He thought of his Mom and her struggle to bring up her twin boys on her own, after their father had run off with a female acrobat from a travelling circus. She was white, whilst he was black, as was Mom, Larry and his twin brother Leroy. His mother had worked all the hours that God sent, to earn money to raise her boys right. She cleaned, she washed, and she scrubbed floors for anyone who would pay, so that her family had a roof over their heads and food to eat. She educated them in the best schools that she could get them to, but while Leroy took to learning, Larry wanted to go his own way. He was smart enough at high school but he had a little bit of a rebellious streak, always wanting to see what was around the next corner, what the options were.

Leroy was the scholar, and his Mom loved him for it. He was top in his class in most subjects and looked set for any career of his choice. After school he would deliver newspapers, wash cars, run errands and generally earn some money to help with the bills. Larry on the other hand tended to disappear when school was over for the day, with his own friends, some of them of quite a dubious nature. He'd come home in the evening with a pocket full of bucks and give most of them to his Mom. Invariably there would be more than Leroy would bring home in a week, which annoyed Leroy no end. When she pressed Larry as to where he had got the cash he would say that he had been helping to move furniture or such like. Whilst she sometimes secretly wondered if he was telling the truth, as long as the cops didn't come knocking at the door, then it all helped.

Leroy questioned his brother many times about his money making activities but he was not forthcoming in any way. In fact when Leroy became insistent that Larry tell him how he was earning the money, they almost came to blows. Larry left education as soon as he could to make his own way in the big world, whilst Leroy stayed on to improve himself and to prepare for life as a black person in his predominantly white home town.

It wasn't long before he was getting in with the wrong company and the foundation for his present difficulties was laid. The day after the heavies arrived at the family's front door looking for him, luckily he was not at home at the time, Larry decided to move out. There had been an almighty row with his brother about Larry bringing shame on the family and so at the age of eighteen he kissed his mother goodbye. He'd shoved his brother aside, the first and only time that he had ever laid hands on him in anger, and stormed out of the house and out of their lives, to seek his fortune, or perhaps it would be his misfortune.

And now tonight it had all come to a climax. It was quite simple really. He had needed some readies and he decided to visit the all night liquor store in the small town of Hurtsburg with a view to relieving the till of few bucks. Hurtsburg was about a half hour drive from where he lived in a mobile home out in the sticks. Larry tended to move his living accommodation around quite a lot, for obvious reasons, and so he found himself not only close to Hurtsburg, but only fifteen miles from his home town.

He parked his old Mercury in the parking lot, turned off the lights, and sat quietly in the darkness, watching for any comings and goings. All was quiet and after a quarter of an hour he decided that it was time to go to work. He got out of the car, leaving the keys in the ignition. He smiled to himself in the darkness, as he thought that it was unlikely that anyone would steal anything as old and battered as his old wreck. He stopped for a moment though, as he recalled the story about the thieves who carried out a robbery but on returning to where they had parked their getaway car, found that someone had stolen it. He took the old Parka jacket from the rear seat and put it on, all the while scanning the area for any possible witnesses to what he was about to do. All was quiet, only the few street lights struggled to penetrate the darkness and of course the light from the front window of the liquor store just visible around the corner from where he had parked the car. He put his hand in the pocket of the old Parka, wondering at the weight, and found the old .44 Magnum hand gun. He hadn't had the coat on for some time and he had forgotten all about the weapon being there. He couldn't remember how he had come by the thing, it had just turned up probably left by one of the guys that he had worked with at some time. Larry had never used a gun on a heist and he almost tossed it into the back of the car, then, as an afterthought he made his big mistake, and put it back in the pocket of the coat. He had a last look around and headed for the shop door. He stopped briefly outside to pull the Parka hood over his head and entered the shop. The door bell clanged loudly announcing his arrival to the attendant and Larry walked briskly to the counter, pulling the Magnum from his pocket. The young guy behind the counter blanched visibly and Larry actually felt quite sorry for him until that is, a steel shutter suddenly crashed down over the front of the cashier's station and a siren started screaming as the attendant dived out of sight behind the counter.

It was about this time that Larry noticed the closed circuit monitor high up on the wall. The camera was showing the car park and right underneath it was his old Mercury. He had been on the screen all the time. His every move had been observed. What a jerk he was! He should have known that the liquor store would have one. His next thought was to flee and just as he was about to turn around and run, the bell clanged on the shop door again as it was kicked open and a voice vaguely familiar, ordered him to put his hands in the air. Larry whirled around, totally forgetting about the gun in his hand, to find a cop in the crouch position, pistol drawn and aiming at him. On seeing Larry's weapon he didn't hesitate and fired a round which hit Larry in the left side of his body, slamming him back against the shop counter. As he twisted around, the hood of the Parka fell back from his head. At the same time the shock of the bullet hitting him caused his right hand to clench on the Magnum and the sound of the shot from the big hand gun was deafening. The policeman, who for some reason had hesitated to fire a second shot, was hurled over backwards as the heavy slug, which could have gone almost anywhere, hit him squarely between the eyes, the top of his head disintegrating in a red mist of bone, brain and blood. Larry clung to the counter, his face a mask of horror, the gun falling from his hand onto the floor. He hadn't even checked that the gun was loaded. He hadn't even aimed it. He had never even fired a gun before. Now he had killed a cop, and who else?

Clutching his side he staggered to the door glancing in horror at the thing on the floor, realising even through his own agony, the true magnitude of what he had just done. As he staggered out onto the sidewalk, he could feel his life blood running everywhere, the pain in his body threatening to bring him to his knees. Somehow he reached the Mercury and got the engine started and drove out of the car park without lights, weaving all over the road in his panic to escape. He had felt sure that there would have been a police back up unit waiting outside the store but the cop had been alone. Larry wished that there had been back up, in which case his double agony would have been over.

Now he was parked up in an old quarry, well away from the scene of the crime, alone with his pain, his misery, and his shame, his life draining away.

His last conscious thought as he took his final breath was for his Mom, and her anguish when she received the news that both of her boys were dead.

Just Deserts

A city in the north of England.

Thanks for taking the time to listen to my story. I need someone to talk to at the moment. I'll start at the beginning or at least one of the beginnings.

My name is John Finlay, Jack to my friends, and I am a professional musician. Well, I play a guitar for money. What I mean is, I am a busker not a beggar. I do not take handouts from the state and I live off what I get from my art such as it is. I pay my bills and I survive. I am thirty eight years old and I live in a city in the north of England. My pitch is right outside the railway station where people are always on the go. My old dog Fred and I would be found there most every day, me sitting on my stool and Fred on his blanket. Old Fred used to get more money than I did, but we were a team and we looked after each other.

About two weeks before Christmas last year, Fred and I were doing our thing. I was doing my John Williams impersonation and Fred curled up close to me, fast asleep. It was about five o'clock, dark and cold with sleet in the air. People were starting to get the Christmas spirit, and my old guitar case lying on the ground in front of me was beginning to attract a few coppers from the passing commuters. I heard some shouting and swearing from a group of youths as they approached.

They were obviously high on something and as they got nearer I caught the aroma from whatever it was that they were smoking. They were passing a couple of joints around and barging through the throng of people whose only wish was to get to the station, get on their train and go home. As they passed me and Fred sitting on the ground, one of them, a big fellow with long blond hair in a ponytail, decided that he wanted some of the money from my guitar case lying in front of me. He scooped a handful of coins and put them in his pocket. I asked him what he thought he was doing. His answer was to kick me in the face, and he then set about me along with the other four or five of his friends. Boots and punches rained in and old Fred woke up and went on the attack, but they kicked him to the ground. I heard 'Longhair' urging his mates to "kill the *******." The last thing I remember was one of them grabbing my guitar and smashing it over my head. The lights went out.

I came round three days later in the City hospital. I was on a drip and a doctor detailed the injuries given to me as Christmas presents by 'Longhair' and his mates. I had a fractured skull and cheekbone, broken nose, four broken ribs and I was not going to play my guitar again for some time because of my broken fingers. The doctor kept the worst news to the last. They had kicked my old friend Fred to death as he fought to protect me.

I cried for some time. He was my only friend.

Belfast 1987

In those days I was Lieutenant John Finlay, 2nd Company, 1st Parachute Regiment. Twenty one years old, young for a First Lieutenant, but I had they said, shown exceptional promise at Sandhurst. My father had been a Major in the 'Rifles' so army life ran in my blood and I took to it like a duck to water.

We were acting on a tip off as to the whereabouts of a top Provisional IRA leader, Sean Galway. Galway was one of the hard men of the Irish Republican Army, a man who led from the front. A man who sent his units out to bomb and kill without any conscience whatsoever. A man who himself, would kill anyone who crossed him, at the drop of a hat. A ruthless disciplinarian, he was both feared and respected by those within his organisation.

We had been trying for a very long time to catch Galway, but his intelligence was as good as ours and either by good luck or judgement, he had always evaded the net. We did catch him once, purely by accident on a routine security sweep and held him for questioning. I had been had been the one in charge of the platoon that pulled him in. He had refused to answer questions. His sneering disdain for the 'Brits' had been hard to take. I had sat in on the interrogation session and he recognised me as the platoon leader. He promised me a short career in the army, or as he put it, 'my card was marked.' Anyway, as usual, a legal representative arrived and because we, at that time had no evidence to hold him, he was released.

Now once again we had information as to his whereabouts. We had sealed off a little side street in North Belfast. The row of two up two down terrace houses had been quietly surrounded in the early hours of the morning. The information was that Galway was in the end house, probably upstairs. The three houses next to Galway's were empty. From the remaining two, we quietly removed the occupants, two elderly couples, to comfortable accommodation.

At exactly 07.00 hours we stormed the house through the front and rear doors. At least two weapons opened up on my lads who returned fire, and a few stun grenades soon silenced the defenders. Two men in the house, one of them wounded, were arrested. I had a look at both of them but neither was our man Galway, and they both denied that he had ever been there. Two of my men were still upstairs collecting evidence. They found a number of firearms, some ammunition and explosives, everything except our target.

Then one of my men spotted a trapdoor on the landing at the top of the stairs. We eventually made it up there and found that in the roof space was a hole, big enough for a man to get through, made in the wall of the adjoining house, and also the next and the next. By the time that we had made our way through to the end house, our progress obviously with great caution, we found that the trapdoor in the end house in the row had been removed and the back door was open. Our target had escaped. Or had he? We had been covering the back and front of the houses and we had seen no one. Could he still be around?

I took two men and went to the other end of the row, posting two others to watch the rear of the house while I covered the front from behind a telegraph pole. The rest of the troop began to work their way along the row of houses clearing them as they came.

As they reached the penultimate house the front door to the end one was flung open and an armed man carrying a rifle sprinted towards a van which had suddenly arrived at the end of an adjacent street. I stepped out, raised my weapon and shouted for the man to halt. He did, but held on to his weapon, an Armalite rifle. He was close enough for me to recognise him as Sean Galway and for him to realise it was me, despite my helmet. He stood for a second, and then raised the weapon. I had no choice now but to open fire. Then to my amazement from off the pavement and between both of us, a young mother wheeling a push chair with a child in it, stepped onto the road. About to pull the trigger, I hesitated, not wanting to harm the civilians. Galway didn't. He opened fire. My flak jacket probably saved my life, but I went down in the road. Just before I passed out I heard him shout,

"Told you I'd get you, Finlay."

My two troopers, joined by the rest of my detachment came under heavy fire from the van which somehow Galway managed to get aboard and escape.

I was taken to an army hospital suffering from a wound to my chest, from a bullet which had unfortunately found a seam in my flak jacket. My right lung had also been damaged. Eighteen months later I was invalided out of the regiment, a promising career had come to an end. I was devastated. I had set my heart on a life in the army.

As they say, life must go on and I concentrated on becoming as fit as I possibly could. Running, lifting weights, everything I could think of to prove the army wrong. I became a fitness fanatic. Slowly but surely over the next couple of years I almost got back to my old self. I worked at anything that I could find and purely by accident, discovered that I had an ear for music in general and guitar playing in particular. With lots of practice over a period of time I became good enough to play in pubs and clubs and I moved around the north of England for several years before settling down.

I kept in touch with my old regiment. Things improved over the years in Northern Ireland and eventually after some time the paramilitaries on both sides stood down. All that is, with the exception of the Real IRA who wanted to continue the armed struggle. It was rumoured that one of its leaders was my old friend Sean Galway, but as time passed he seemed to have disappeared from sight and nothing was heard from him. It was thought that he had been disposed of, the victim of an internal feud perhaps. But I still felt that one day he and I would meet again.

North of England early 2006

My recovery from the beating handed out by 'Longhair' and his friends was good. My fitness helped me a great deal and I healed quickly. The doctors at the hospital noticed the scarring on my chest and so I had to explain how it had happened. The police were sympathetic and kept me informed as to how their investigations were going on.

One day in the middle of February I received a phone call asking me to go to police headquarters. When I arrived, the officer in charge of the case informed me that several young men had been arrested, and asked if I could formally identify them as being my attackers.

I was taken to a room which had a large window in one wall, through which I could see, seated at a table opposite two interviewing officers, 'Longhair'. I had no problem whatsoever identifying him to the officer in charge; I would never forget him until the day I died. The police officer told me that he had been positively identified by quite a few witnesses as had some of his cronies. He already had a criminal record for GBH and for drug offences. Police had raided his house, which although he was only twenty three years old, he owned outright, no mortgage, nothing, all paid for.

His name they told me was Patrick Galway. I looked more closely at him through the window of the interview room. I was assured that whilst I could see and hear him, he was oblivious to our presence on the other side of the wall. Then as I listened, I became aware of his voice which still had a slight Belfast accent.

I now became a lot more interested in what was going on next door. 'Longhair' was asked about his next of kin. His parents he said were dead but he had an uncle who was quite frail and living in a Nursing Home on the outskirts of the city. His name apparently was Anthony Mulhearn.

My mind was now working overtime. Was Mulhearn really Mulhearn or someone else? I was by now fully convinced that 'Longhair' was the son of Sean Galway. His mannerisms and his looks were very similar. I could never forget or mistake them.

The officer in charge assured me that 'Longhair' and his cronies would be sent to prison for a long time, for assault, dealing in hard drugs, robbery and possession of firearms. They would be bothering no one for a long time. Apparently the best lawyers that could be found had been assigned to the case at great expense, but such was the evidence against them, it was an open and shut case. Police did not know who had funded the defence lawyers. I could have hazarded a guess but I decided to hold my tongue for a little longer. Having signed my statement I was allowed to leave, my mind already planning my next move.

Next day I removed a wooden box from the bottom of my wardrobe. I opened it and took out my old service pistol, a 9mm Browning. Its well oiled metal gleamed dully in the light from the bedroom window. I loaded the magazine and replaced it in the butt of the pistol, put on the safety catch and tucked the gun inside the waist band of my trousers in the hollow of the small of my back. I put on my best jacket, left my flat and caught the bus to the village where the nursing home was. The bus stop was actually right outside the front gate.

It was mid afternoon when I rang the bell on the front door. It was opened by a nurse in uniform, a name badge was pinned to it, proclaiming her to be Margaret Simpson, Deputy Matron. I asked if I could visit Mr Mulhearn, whom I had not seen for some time and who was an old acquaintance of mine. She was quite chatty and remarked casually that it was usually his Irish relatives who visited him and not English people. She went on to tell me that he had lived in the nursing home for five or six years, longer in fact than she had worked there. He'd had a series of strokes and was now totally paralysed and unable to speak. As I was an old friend I could visit him for a few minutes. I asked if there was anything that he needed and she assured me that everything was provided for him including the cost of his care package, by his large family circle, who it seemed were very well off.

She led me down a long corridor and knocked gently on a room door and ushered me inside.

"Visitor Anthony," she called. "You can have ten minutes, Mr?"

"Thank you Nurse," I replied ignoring her request for my name and went into the room.

She left, closing the door gently behind her.

I stood for a moment looking around the room. A high backed wing chair faced away from me towards a large television which was showing a western movie, the sound turned down low. I walked towards the chair, removing my gun from under my jacket but keeping it out of sight. I looked at the man sitting in there. All his hair had fallen out. His skin was pale, wax like and his fingers twisted. One side of his face had dropped, paralysed by the strokes he had suffered, saliva dribbling from the side of his mouth. The only sign of life was in his eyes. They looked at me blankly for a moment and I watched them as recognition dawned. They came alive, radiating a malevolence that I could almost feel. This apparition before me, this excuse for a man was Sean Galway.

"Hello Sean," I said "remember me? I've been looking for you for a long time." The look in his eyes told me that he remembered very well.

I brought out my pistol, eased off the safety catch and put the barrel to his head. I almost pulled the trigger. The eyes for a moment showed fear, and as I hesitated the look changed to pleading. I could almost hear his thoughts begging me to shoot. His eyes were saying, "Put me out of my misery." I suddenly realised that would be too kind. I put the safety catch back on and returned the gun to my waist band.

"You want me to end it for you Sean? You, the man who had sympathy for no-one. You know what? I hope that you live to be a thousand."

I turned and walked towards the room door. I looked back at the thing in the chair. It was weeping.

I went home and rang my old friends in army intelligence and told them the story. Some of Sean Galway's so called relatives would be getting a call. For the first time in years I had got the monkey off my back.

Thank you again for listening to my story.

I was a man

As I sit and watch the world go by
each little thing is of interest.
Watching someone hoovering, dusting,
switching on the telly.
I WAS A MAN.

Sometimes I think I don't exist
not seen, not heard,
ignored by all, unless by superhuman effort
I raise my hand or catch their eye.
I WAS A MAN.

In my youth I fought for king and country.
I married, was a father to my children,
brought them up well,
sheltered them from harm.
I WAS A MAN.

Now at three score years and ten
a stroke has laid me low.
From being someone who mattered,
I feel I no longer truly exist.
I WAS A MAN.

But wait, someone speaks,
They ask for my opinion.
They see the spark of life in my eyes.
They look deep, beyond the frail shadow that is before them
And they understand.
OH JOY, I AM A MAN.

Francis Brown

The Old Rocking Chair

Mary and Tom lived on the outskirts of Tewkesbury. Their home was a little bungalow in one of those idyllic tree lined avenues: you know the ones, a mixture of semis and large elegant houses that had been built in the nineteen thirties. The sort of place where neighbours were nice to each other and the wives popped into each other's houses for morning coffee. The men would go off to work each day and return home at the same time every evening to find their meal on the table and their homes as clean as new pins. The avenue was a veritable model of suburban respectability.

They had been married for almost thirty years, and their two sons, William and Robert, were both married, working and living abroad with their young families. Both of their sons had two children each but as they lived so far away it was very rarely that they got home on a visit to see their parents.

Mary and Tom loved their children and their families dearly but they loved each other also, and as long as they knew that their lads and their families were alright, they were both content in each other's company.

Mary had a part time job in the local library and Tom worked in the Housing Department of the local council, a job he had held virtually since leaving school, progressing through the ranks to his present executive role.

They were at the stage in their marriage were they felt extremely comfortable with each other. Sometimes they seemed to know in advance what the other was about to say or do, and on occasion would fall about laughing when, after a period of companionable silence both would start to say the same thing at the same time. All of this did not mean that things were dull or hum drum, in fact it was just the opposite, as they always seemed to have lots to do. They went everywhere together, especially enjoying regular holidays in Spain and around the Mediterranean. They also enjoyed weekends in various parts of rural England, and shared many interests. In fact there didn't seem to be enough hours in the day to do all the things that they wanted to do.

As with most marriages, or when two people live together for a long time, just when they think that they know everything that there is to know about their partner, something new would emerge out of the blue. In this respect Mary and Tom were no different from anyone else.

One evening after tea when the washing up was all finished and put away, they sat down on the old sofa in front of the fire, and Tom put his arm around Mary's shoulder and she snuggled up against him.

"Tom," she said.

"Yes Mary?" Tom said looking sideways at her, an eyebrow raised questioningly.

"Do you know what I would like?"

"And what would that be my beloved?" Tom asked, grinning wickedly.

Mary punched him playfully on the shoulder "Behave yourself, husband. I would like a rocking chair."

"What? One of those things that old grannies sit on?" Tom asked grinning broadly.

"Yes" said Mary, "if it comes to that, I am an old granny, just like you're an old granddad."

"Less of the old," laughed Tom. "What do you want with a rocking chair? Is this something new you've taken a fancy for?"

"No," said Mary, "I've wanted one for a long time. My grandmother used to have one and I would sit on her knee and she would rock me on it until I fell asleep. I always felt so safe there. I suppose I always would have liked a rocking chair but I never seemed to get round to looking for one."

"Well," said Tom, giving her a squeeze "if that's what you would like, then we will look for a rocking chair for you my little cherub, but I hope you realise that it's going to cost you," and he gave her a playful hug.

Mary put her arms around his neck and kissed him.

"How about something on account big boy?"

She had decided that she wanted an old rocking chair, not one of those modern things all mahogany, moquette and springs. So over the next few weeks they answered adverts in the local newspapers, visited second hand furniture stores but unfortunately, none of the chairs that they saw was the one that Mary was looking for. The weeks drifted into months and Tom had all but forgotten about Mary's rocking chair. Then, one Saturday morning they went to a local car boot sale, and as they strolled up and down the rows of tables, laden with every conceivable second hand article that its owner had no further use for, Tom was suddenly aware that Mary was tugging at his sleeve.

"Look," she said, "look at that!"

"Look at what?" asked Tom. "There are millions of things everywhere."

"Over there, behind that blue Volvo estate." Mary said. "It's a rocking chair! Can we go over and have a look? Ask how much it is." Mary said excitedly.

Mary took Tom's hand as they threaded their way through the throng of bargain hunters until they reached the back of the Volvo. Apart from the chair there didn't seem to be much else for sale. There was a small square tarpaulin spread out on the ground with a few bits and pieces laid out on top of it. The owner appeared to be an old gentleman, probably in his late seventies or even early eighties. Mary went over and stood in front of him.

"Excuse me," Mary said, "is that your rocking chair?"

"It is indeed young lady," the old chap answered with a sad little smile.

"Is it for sale?" Mary asked shyly.

"Aye it is," said the old man.

"May I sit in it?" she asked excitedly.

"Please do," he told her.

Mary stepped over the corner of the tarpaulin and reaching behind her for the arms of the chair, lowered herself carefully into the seat. A big smile of pleasure lit up her face as she tried a few tentative rocks. She looked up at Tom who himself was grinning broadly and said excitedly, "I think this is the one I've been looking for Tom."

Tom turned to the old gentleman who had been watching the proceedings. "How much would you like for the rocking chair?" he asked.

"Well," said the old chap, "I'll give you a little bit of its history, if you would like to hear it," and he waited expectantly until Tom and Mary both nodded their agreement. "It belonged to my wife," he continued, "and before that to her mother. My mother in law was a lovely lady, a good wife and mother, and although she had nine children she looked after them all equally well. When all her children got married and had children of their own she looked after them too. Mrs Brett, that was her name, and I never called her by anything else. We always showed respect for our elders in those days I suppose." He didn't speak for a moment or two, his thoughts somewhere in the past. Then he continued, "She always wore a long black dress with a snow white collar and apron and a pair of shiny black lace up ankle boots that would gladden the heart of a company sergeant major." He stopped for a moment as though gathering his thoughts again. Tom and Mary stood silently, not wishing to interrupt his reverie. They watched the old man's face, his expression changing as a series of memories flitted through his mind. Then he continued, "She liked a bottle of stout now and again, for medicinal purposes you understand," and he gave them a conspiratorial wink. "She used to smoke a clay pipe," he continued, "used some sort of aromatic tobacco that she acquired from somewhere. She would sit in that old rocking chair with her glass of stout, get her pipe going, and rock gently for long enough."

"We always knew that when old Mrs Brett was in her rocking chair, all was right with the world, because if there was work to do, or if someone was poorly, she never rested until all was well again. When she died, it passed to my wife Anne, but she could never seem to get comfortable with it, but wouldn't get rid of it either."

"Why is she selling it now?" asked Tom, almost biting his tongue as the answer suddenly stared him in the face.

The old man's lip quivered as he replied. "She died almost a month ago. I've been clearing a lot of her stuff out to the family and charity shops and this is all that I have got left." and he indicated the few items on the blue tarpaulin which included the old rocking chair.

"How much would you like for the chair?" Tom asked quietly, deeply touched by the old man's story.

The old fellow looked from Tom to Mary, who was now sitting absolutely still in the chair, her lip trembling just a little, and with just a hint of a tear on her cheek.

"Well," he said, "I'll tell you what. I've seen the way your little woman has taken to it and I would like it to go to a good home, somewhere that it will be enjoyed as it used to be. Please take it with my good wishes."

Tom attempted to interrupt the old chap and took out his wallet in order to give him some money, but he wouldn't hear of it. He packed up his bits and pieces on the tarpaulin and put them in the back of the Volvo. He climbed into the driver's seat and closed the door. Winding down the window as he started the engine, he leaned out and simply said, "Thank you," and drove off.

Mary and Tom, to say the least, were gob smacked. They looked at the throng of people milling around the nearby stalls, but no one was paying them the slightest bit of attention, so there was nothing else to do but to take the old rocking chair home.

The next day, Mary cleaned and polished the old chair until it shone like new, and installed it in the living room by the window. Every day whenever she had finished her house work she would sit and rock in it for a little while. She told Tom that it was extremely therapeutic and that she usually finished up having a little doze.

The months went by and she began to have problems with her health. Nothing too bad at first, but things got progressively worse. She was never one to grumble or complain, but Tom was worried out of his mind, and managed eventually, to get her to see her GP. After an examination, the doctor suggested to Mary that to be on the safe side, he would arrange for her to go to her local hospital to have some tests and X rays carried out.

When the day for her tests arrived, Tom took the day off work and accompanied Mary to the hospital. Time dragged as he sat in the waiting room. He prayed silently to himself that there was nothing seriously wrong, he just could not visualise life without her.

After what seemed an eternity, probably more like an hour and a half, a nurse came out to the waiting area and took Tom through to the consultant's office. Mary was sitting in a chair in front of his desk, still wearing a dressing gown.

"Please sit down Tom," he said smiling reassuringly and indicating a chair beside Mary. Tom sat down and automatically took her hand in his. The consultant looked at Mary before continuing. It was obvious to Tom that they had already been discussing things before he had arrived.

"To bring you up to date Tom, we've done a scan and X-rays, and the results seem to confirm what your GP suspected. We think that Mary has a tumour. I and other colleagues, whom I have called in, feel that it is in her best interests that we deal with it as soon as possible."

Tom bit back the panic that gripped his heart and it must have shown momentarily on his face as Mary squeezed his hand and tried a brave little smile. She wasn't one for breaking down.

"I'm sorry Tom, I asked the doctor to tell us both what was happening. I felt that between us that we would be strong enough to deal with it." Tom nodded dumbly. Suddenly he felt a strength growing within him and he sat up straight in his chair, Mary's hand still tightly clasped in his.

"Right doctor, what happens now," Tom asked positively.

"I want you both to go home, and the hospital will notify you as soon as possible when we can do the operation. Sometimes we get cancellations so it could be anytime soon. Mary will come into hospital on the day before surgery. The positive side is that her condition is operable and we have a very high success rate, plus the fact that we may have got it in good time."

Tom looked at Mary's pale face, gave her a smile and squeezed her hand again.

"See, it's going to be alright." Mary nodded.

The doctor rose from his chair, opened the consulting room door and called in the nurse who had shown Tom in the room. "Right Mary," he said brightly, "Nurse will take you off to get dressed and Tom will be waiting for you when you're ready."

Mary went off with the nurse and the door closed. The doctor walked around the desk and put his hand on Tom's shoulder. Tom looked him straight in the eye.

"What's it really like doctor? There's more to it than that isn't there?"

"It's quite bad Tom, The tumour is quite well advanced. If I can get Mary through the operation, then we have a good chance. So let's pray that all goes well. You take her home now and we will be in touch as soon as possible."

The next few days were the longest and the shortest that they had ever known. Tom stayed home from work and tried to be positive, bright and cheerful, to keep Mary's spirits up and her thoughts away from her impending operation.

Inevitably the day came for Mary to go into hospital, luckily sooner rather than later, as there had been a cancellation. She went into a little ward of her own, and Tom was allowed to spend the whole day with her. He even spent the night dozing in a chair at the end of her bed. Next morning Mary seemed quite calm as she waited for her pre-med, even trying to make a joke or two, but Tom could see that it was purely for his sake. The nurses came to take her down to the operating theatre and he was allowed to accompany her to the little ante room where she would be given her anaesthetic. He took her small hand in his, tears coursing down his face.

"I love you Mary," he said.

Mary closed her eyes and tears squeezed out from between her eyelids, as the anaesthetist inserted the needle into the back of her hand. Her eyes full of uncertainty, fear, and terror even, turned to Tom's as she fought the anaesthetic, but slowly her eyes closed again.

The surgeon who came out of the theatre looked closely at her, then at Tom, and nodded.

"We'll do our best," he said. "You have a seat in the waiting room if you feel that you don't want to go home, and we'll let you know when it's over. I must warn you, we will be some time."

Tom sat in the waiting room, his mind in turmoil. He prayed, he walked about, he sat, he stood, he couldn't settle his body or his thoughts for a minute. When anyone came through the swing doors from the direction of the operating theatre, he would look up expectantly, but usually the nurse or orderly would walk straight past him.

Then about five hours after Mary had gone into theatre, the surgeon came through the door. He was wearing his green gown and cap and carried his face mask in his hand. Tom leapt from his chair and went to meet him, his thoughts so jumbled with worry that he could hardly speak coherently.

"How....? Is she all right?"

The surgeon took his arm and led him to a small room with a table and a couple of easy chairs, and closed the door.

He motioned for Tom to sit in one of the chairs, whilst he sat in the other. Tom could hardly contain himself as he waited for the man to speak. He tried to read his face for some clue as to what news he was about to give.

"Well Tom," he finally said, "we've done what we can. Mary's going to be a little while coming out of the anaesthetic. It's all down to her now. I would suggest that you go off home now, get some rest, and come back sometime tomorrow morning. She will go into intensive care for at least twenty four hours, and in the mean time, if there is any change for the worse in her condition, we have your telephone number."

"May I see her before I go?" Tom asked.

"Only for a minute," the surgeon replied, "and don't be put off by all the tubes and drips. She won't know that you are there, she's still in a pretty deep sleep."

"Many thanks for all that you've done for Mary." Tom said. The surgeon smiled,

"I'm sure that she has a good chance of coming through all this. We'll look after her. Now remember, just a couple of minutes," and he walked off in the direction of the theatre again.

Tom entered the recovery room. Two young nurses were busy around Mary's bed. They stopped what they were doing and stood aside as he approached. Mary's face was like a death mask, a faint sheen of perspiration covered her face. Tubes were coming from her nose and mouth, whilst a tube from a drip on a stand was taped to the back of her hand. He walked slowly over to the bed his eyes fixed on his wife's face, and took her hand in his. It was limp and hot.

He bent and kissed her forehead, turned quickly and left the room, tears welling from his eyes. He walked in a daze to the entrance to the hospital noticing absently that it was growing dark as he went to the taxi rank and got into the first cab in the line. Tom didn't remember giving the driver his address. He did remember giving the man some money and then finding himself standing in the gathering darkness outside his front gate.

He looked at the darkened windows, the first time that he could ever remember coming back to an empty home. Mary had always been there to welcome him at the front door, the lights on, a hot meal ready and a cheerful fire in the grate. Now the little bungalow was as black as the crypt. He unlocked the front door and stepped into the hallway closing the door behind him.

He didn't switch on the light, he didn't have to. He had come in here a thousand times, all of them happier than now. The door to the living room was ajar and he went inside. He felt totally exhausted, his mind numb with worry. He still didn't switch on the light; instead he took off his jacket, a birthday present from Mary, draped it over the back of the sofa, then, slumping down stretched out in the darkness. He lay there listening. The little bungalow was silent too, as though it shared his worries for Mary. Slowly tiredness overcame him and he drifted off into a fitful sleep, his tortured mind taking the opportunity to rest.

He became aware of being awake sometime later. He laid there, eyes closed, as the events of the past couple of days returned to torment him. He would go and ring the hospital. He suddenly felt heartened that at least the hospital had not rung him. Then he began to feel guilty, perhaps he had slept so soundly that he had not heard the telephone.

Suddenly, his eyes still closed, he became aware of a strong perfume in the room. Was that furniture polish? No, more like a fragrant pipe tobacco. At the same time he could hear, perhaps in his mind, a rhythmic creaking. He cracked open one eye to see a shaft of early morning sunlight streaming through a partially open venetian blind. Little motes of dust drifted through the golden beams, and something else, tendrils of a smoke like substance drifted through the rays. Tom's eyes now took in the old chair, gently rocking back and forth, creaking in time.

Suddenly he remembered what the old gentleman had said about his mother in law, Mrs Brett, who only sat down on her rocking chair, to enjoy her glass of stout and her pipe, when all the work was done and everyone was on the mend.

And Mary was.

A Fairy Tale
(of our time)

PART I
HARD TIMES

Down in the woods, the largest gathering of fairies, elves, goblins, leprechauns, nymphs and assorted little people ever seen in the history of the Great Glade, was taking place. They had come from all over the kingdom at the request of Her Imperial Majesty, Tallulah the Fairy Queen. The last time such a gathering had been called by Her Majesty, was so long ago that no one, except the Queen, was old enough to remember when it had occurred. What they knew of that gathering was that it had been at the time of the Great Forest fire, when most of the Great Forest had been destroyed. The fire had been started by a lightning bolt from the Kingdom above the clouds, with great loss of life among the little folk. Tales of the devastation had been handed down from generation to generation and was part of their folklore. The total destruction of their habitat had been catastrophic and only the kindness of little people in other parts of the Great Kingdom had saved many from extinction. Now a similar Great Gathering had been called by Her Majesty and no-one except the Queen seemed to know why.

The fact that the reason for the Imperial Summons was not known, did nothing to dampen the enthusiasm of the masses of the population of Queen Tallulah's kingdom for a get together and a bit of a knees up. The day was warm and sunny and everyone was in their best bib and tucker. In the absence of any news to the contrary, all of the little people were set for a happy and glorious day out, as was their wont.

As they waited for their Queen to arrive, improvised entertainment was quickly organised. First of all the leprechauns from across the Wide River danced, sang and cavorted about, to the great delight and vociferous approval of all who got close enough to see them in action. They in turn were followed by a group of Cornish Piskies, led by a little lady piskie answering to the name of Joan the Wad, who juggled with pots and plates, and organised a competition to see who could eat the most Cornish pasties without being sick. This was won by a gnome from Nuneaton called Norman, who, because of the amount of pasties he had consumed, had to be carried off by six of his mates, to great applause, as his legs wouldn't support him.

Next to perform was an elf from Northumbria, who was a porter with the National Elf Service, who gave a superb demonstration of riding a two wheeled unicycle. His performance only ended when he wobbled off course and collided with the Fairy Godmother, knocking her over, and bending her magic wand into a 'U' shape. She was so incensed that she pointed the afore mentioned, bent, magic wand at the poor old elf, muttered a magic spell under her breath, and to the delight of the watching multitude who thought it was deliberate, turned herself into a frog.

The day was now truly beautiful, a typical English, early summers day. The sun shone brightly from out of a clear blue sky and the southerly breeze was light and warm. The trees were showing off their new green mantle of leaves, and the grass on the floor of the Great Glade rippled like wavelets on a lake, as the gentle breeze passed over it, ruffling the yellow buttercups. Her Majesty's subjects were dressed in their best outfits, all of them brightly coloured and including every hue of the rainbow.

The huge crowd of spectators were by now thoroughly enjoying themselves. Next on the agenda was an impromptu formation flypast by a twelve strong squadron of nymphs, trailing multi coloured smoke. They looped and rolled, climbed almost out of sight and then diving down towards the crowd, only pulling up at the last moment, and thrilling the spectators. They received a huge ovation as they flew off. Everyone was still buzzing with excitement when, suddenly, the air was rent by the deafening sound of the Great Battle Horn of Her Majesty's Chamber Orchestra. This Great Battle Horn was reportedly the length of three large cows stood end to end, and had been a gift to Queen Tallulah from the Crown Prince of the Royal Gnomes of Zurich in the far off land of the mountains in the sky. The Crown Prince kind of fancied Her Imperial Majesty, but there had been two problems with this arrangement. One, she didn't fancy him and two, there was no-one in the whole kingdom who could play the blasted thing. So, faced with having the Great Battle Horn returned to him, and looking a right nana, the Crown Prince allowed one of the best horn blowers in his personal orchestra, to be seconded to the Queen as her Great Battle Horn player for as long as she needed him. At this moment he was earning his keep as he signalled the imminent arrival of Her Imperial Majesty.

As yet, none of the gathering of Her Majesty's subjects had an inkling as to why they had been summoned, but most agreed that it must be relatively important, and so until she told them why, they would continue to enjoy their day out.

Then, at the far end of the Great Glade there was a commotion and, the huge crowd began to divide into two halves as the Queen's escort began to clear a way through the mass of loyal subjects, many of whom had never seen Her Imperial Majesty before. As her carriage approached the large marquee at the head of the Great Glade, the cheers from the ecstatic throng reached a deafening crescendo. The Royal Coach, finished in burnished gold, was dazzling to the eyes of the beholders in the bright sunlight, and some of her subjects were visibly overcome by the occasion. It eventually came to a stop slightly past the marquee and the two coachmen were seen to be struggling to bring it to a halt. The reason became apparent when it was noticed that it was being drawn by a team of twelve snow white wallabies which had been trained to hop in unison. These were a gift from the people of Queensland, a country at the other side of the Great Orb, where the sun went every night. Unfortunately, whilst the wallabies hopped in unison, the journey in the Golden Coach had not been smooth for her Majesty. In fact, as she staggered from the coach, with the Imperial Crown hanging over one ear, she was looking decidedly pale. She was quickly escorted inside the marquee for a lie down and a cuppa, and was heard to say in a very loud voice, that an alternative form of transport for the journey home had better be found, or else!

After a short interval, her Majesty's General Factotum emerged from the huge marquee and onto the raised stage in front, and called the crowd to order. A goblin, tall for his height, he was dressed in green knee breeches, a bright red braided jacket with gold buttons down the front, and wearing black wellington boots. On his head, which was totally devoid of hair, he wore a large pointed hat, which had a three foot long feather sticking out of it. He stood there for a minute or two waiting for the crowd to quieten down, and then, in a voice that carried to the far extremes of the multitude, he announced,

"Her Imperial Majesty, Queen Tallulah the Fairy Queen, ruler of all she surveys and many other places that she doesn't."

Her Majesty's subjects, unused to the protocol involved during such occasions, bowed their heads, tugged forelocks, bent the knee, knelt on the ground, or prostrated themselves, as the mood took them, each demonstrating their allegiance to their sovereign in their own way.

When Queen Tallulah finally appeared she seemed quite moved by the spectacle, certainly she still looked quite pale and a little unsteady on her feet, whether this was as a result of the affection shown to her by her loyal subjects or the residue of her journey in the state coach, drawn by twelve snow white wallabies trained to hop in unison. The crowd then stood and gave Her Majesty three rousing cheers, which she acknowledged with a wave of her hand. They then commenced to give their Sovereign another three cheers, and only when all this had been repeated several times and the whole performance seemed to be getting out of hand, did the General Factotum have the bright idea of signalling to the Great Battle Horn player to call the assembly to order. Bear in mind that no-one, not even the Fairy Queen, was aware of the impromptu performance that was about to be unleashed upon the gathering. So, when this little Swiss musician, with his mighty Battle Horn, the length of three cows stood end to end, suddenly let out a series of deafening toots, all hell broke loose. The Queen leapt about six feet into the air, landing on top of the General Factotum, ramming his hat down over his ears, both of them finishing in a tangled heap on the floor. The twelve snow white wallabies, trained to hop in unison, suddenly took off, *none* of them hopping in unison, towing the Golden Coach behind them, unfortunately all in different directions, much to the chagrin of the two coachmen trying to steer the thing. It was last seen careering off in a southerly direction at a high rate of knots.

The gnome from Nuneaton called Norman, yes, he of the Cornish pasties, had a nasty accident when he awoke to the sound of the Battle Horn. He had to be rescued from half way up a fifty foot high pine tree, and requiring a new pair of trousers. A nymph called Nancy and two of her friends who were in the process of taking up a collection in aid of the Homeless Shepherds Society, were totally bowled over by an incensed warthog, known to his friends as Cecil. Now Cecil having heard the noise made by the Battle Horn, thought that his territory was being invaded by a whole herd of foreign warthogs, and he proceeded to charge around through the panic stricken mass, determined to sort out the infiltrators. Unfortunately for the unicyclist with the two wheeled bike, the elf from Northumbria who was a porter with the National Elf Service, Cecil spotted him and, in the absence of the herd of foreign warthogs, decided that he would do instead. Now Cecil was quick, but the guy on the bike was no slouch either, at least, not after he spotted the enraged warthog heading for him, tusks glinting in the sunshine. Fear lent him wings and his little legs were just a blur as he thrust mightily on the pedals. The elf, with Cecil inches from the back wheel of the bike, burst out of the crowd into the open meadow. The crowd was now totally ignoring the din made by the Great Battle Horn, cheering madly at the spectacle of the race between the elf and the enraged warthog, as the two chased madly around the meadow. A few pixies and the leprechauns from across the Wide River were placing bets as to who would win. The elf opened up a slight gap and as Cecil appeared to be tiring the elf, with a desperate look over his shoulder, headed for the trees that marked the start of the Great Forest. He almost made it but Cecil spotted what he was up to and decided to head him off at the pass. Unfortunately for the elf and Cecil as it turned out, about six feet from the safety of the trees the chain came off the bike. The elf suddenly took a flyer over the handlebars, landing in a flurry of grass and sods, just as Cecil launched himself, managing to get his head stuck under the crossbar and finishing up wearing the bike around his neck. The elf desperately threw himself sideways as Cecil, suddenly realising that he was heading at high speed straight for two very large trees standing quite close together, thundered past. Cecil was not daft, and he realised in a nano second that he was not going to be able to stop before he came to the trees, and his little piggy type brain computed a course to take him between them. Brilliant, apart from one little error! Unfortunately for him his little piggy type brain forgot to include the bicycle around his neck in the equation and whilst his head passed quite safely between the trees at a rate of knots, the rest of him did not, at least not in the way it would have done had he not had the bike around his neck. The bicycle frame came to an abrupt halt, but somehow Cecil's momentum shot him right out the other side and he came to rest head first, quite suddenly, against the trunk of a large oak tree. Then he just seemed to lose all interest in the proceedings. The elf made the most of his good fortune and scampered back to lose himself in the centre of the crowd, before Cecil came round again. His return was accompanied by the cheers of the leprechauns who had won their bets on the outcome of this race with Cecil, now reclining at the foot of the oak tree.

By this time Her Majesty had retired once more into the marquee for another cup of tea and the General Factotum was once again trying to bring some semblance of order to the proceedings. He was having to shout at the top of his voice above the racket caused by the Great Battle Horn player. After a couple of minutes he lost all self control, his patience had totally expired. With his pointed hat now a crumpled mess, and its three foot long feather a tangled wreck following Her Majesty's landing on top of him, he stumped across the platform in his wellies. His little goblin face was twisted with fury and as red as the tail light on the elf's two wheeled unicycle.

Now the object of his ire, the Great Battle Horn player from Zurich, was delighted to have been given another chance to show off his skill as a musician and carried on playing at full volume, totally unaware of the mayhem he was causing. Right in front of the platform, the leprechauns who had been celebrating their winnings from the pixies, and who would bet on two flies crawling up a wall, now opened another book on the result of the coming confrontation.

The General Factotum marched up behind the musician, who was still blissfully unaware of any problems and mistaking the cheers from the leprechauns as a sign of their appreciation of his skill, redoubled his efforts. The GF's welly making contact with his nether regions resulted in a strangled howl, partially from the musician and partly from his instrument and was followed immediately by a deafening silence. The crowd cheered and shouted their approval as the GF, suddenly finding himself in the spotlight, his anger assuaged by his sudden popularity, took a bow at the front of the platform. Meanwhile the Great Battle Horn Player had managed to remove the mouthpiece of the afore mentioned Great Battle Horn from the back of his throat. He produced his Swiss army knife from his little pocket in his lederhosen and selecting the largest and sharpest blade there, marched purposely up behind the General Factotum, still wallowing in his new found popularity. He inserted the razor sharp blade in the seam of his red braided jacket and with a quick upward thrust, ripped the jacket up to the collar. He folded up his little knife, bowed to the audience and marched briskly from the platform in a huff.

The General Factotum meanwhile, suddenly felt a draught, and reaching round behind him, discovered that he was now the proud owner of a swallow tailed jacket. Realising what had happened, he was about to go off to seek retribution from the musician, when the voice of Her Majesty was heard, calling him. Hastily clutching the ends of his jacket together behind his back, he scuttled off the platform to thunderous applause, and went inside the marquee to attend his Queen.

Five minutes later he reappeared; his jacket hastily repaired using half a dozen clothes pegs to hold the seam together, and called on the assembled throng to come to order. The crowd hushed expectantly, as Her Imperial Majesty, Tallulah, Queen of all the Fairies, looking quite relaxed, and fortified most likely with a little libation, glided regally on to the platform. Her loyal subjects applauded with great enthusiasm and for a moment the General Factotum feared a repeat of the first appearance of Her Majesty before her people. Luckily when she raised her hands to appeal for silence, they obeyed immediately.

"My loyal subjects," she began, "I have summoned you here today to the Great Glade, in order to bring to your attention, a calamity of outstanding proportions which has befallen our kingdom." A murmur of concern ran through the crowd. They hushed again as their Queen raised her tiny hands to appeal for silence and waited for her to continue.

"As we all know," she began, "the economic climate in the world of the giants is in chaos. There are no jobs, people have run out of money, and the Black Gold as they call it, is now almost beyond price. She paused for a moment to let this news sink in. A loud voice from the centre of the crowd was heard to shout,

"What has that got to do with us, Your Majesty?" and there were mutters of agreement from several areas of the crowd. Her Majesty raised her hands again pleadingly, and quiet returned once more.

"Unfortunately for ourselves, the little people of this great world, it has everything to do with us. We have never experienced famine, unemployment or poverty. Do you agree?" A murmur of grudging assent was heard from the gathering. "And why do you think that is?" The crowd was silent.

"I will tell you why," the Queen continued, "it is because we, the little people, have traded with the giants for as long as I can remember and we have been well rewarded for our hard work."

"What do they take from us?" cried the voice from the crowd. Again there were mutterings of agreement.

Her Majesty continued, "Who buys the Mead from our distilleries in the hills? Where do the Liquorice Allsorts go that are produced in our assembly plant in the Great Forest, not to mention the machines that we manufacture for injecting jam into doughnuts? What about the factory that produces the keys for the corned beef tins, used all over the known world? These are just the tip of the iceberg. We also train the honey bees not only to gather honey, but also to deliver it to the hives of the Giants. All of these things bring rewards to our treasury and have contributed to the wealth of our people over the years. Normally when things go wrong financially in the Land of the Giants, believe it or not, we the little people have, time and time again, been their saviour. This had not been common knowledge either in our kingdom or theirs and has been governed over by our learned officials who know about these things. And so, my loyal subjects, do you now see why we are concerned by the problems in the Land of the Giants?"

Just then there was a commotion in the crowd and a large fairy dressed in rather faded denim jacket and trousers, pushed his way through the crush and stood directly in front of the Her Majesty. The General Factotum looked a little worried and prepared to place himself between the rough looking fairy and his Queen, but all was well when the big fairy knelt before Her Majesty and tugged his forelock.

"Permission to speak, Your Majesty?" he said. The General Factotum looked quizzically at his Queen and she acknowledged his unspoken question with an almost imperceptible nod of her head.

"You may speak, but first of all, what is your name and what do you do?"

The big fairy stood up and looked the Queen straight in the eye.

"My name is Egbert, Your Majesty, and I am your most faithful servant. I am a Birkenhead fairy and I am shop steward of the T.H.U.G.S." he said, spelling out the letters.

The Queen returned his look and asked, "What are the T.H.U.G.S.?"

Egbert again looked at the Queen and replied, "The letters stand for Trolls and Hobgoblins Undergraduates Society, Ma'am."

"Very well, er, Egbert, what would you like to say?"

"Well Your Majesty, it's more of a question really. You say that we the little people have helped the Giant's economy many times in the past. Why can we not do so this time?" The crowd nodded in agreement and murmured approvingly in support.

"An excellent question, Egbert. That brings me directly to our next bit of bad news. In the past we always had our reserves of capital, in short, our Horn of Plenty. Our secret stash against bad times! Most ordinary people think of it as a fairy story. Believe me it is no fairy story. It exists, or at least it did, until the last full moon.

I refer to the Great Crock of Gold, the one at the end of the rainbow. Only a handful of people, those who look after our economy, are truly aware of its existence and its whereabouts. When we became aware of the financial turmoil in the Land of the Giants, we decided to remove enough gold to replenish their economy as we had secretly done many times before. Like the Horn of Plenty, the Crock of Gold always replenishes itself and no matter how much or how often we have to borrow from it, it is always full. Unfortunately this time when we went to remove a quantity of the precious metal we discovered that the crock had been stolen, placing not only the Giant's economy, but more importantly our own, in jeopardy. Does that answer your question, Egbert?"

The big Birkenhead fairy nodded his head, "Yes thank you, Your Majesty, now may I ask another?"

"Ask away, Egbert," she said.

"What are we going to do about it, Ma'am?" Again murmurs of approval from the crowd.

"Good question again, Egbert. Well, our plan is to enlist a small group of our best people, who will be empowered to take whatever steps, preferably quick ones, necessary to bring the perpetrators of this crime to justice, in order to restore financial stability to all. We, by we, I mean our small group of leading citizens who govern our little kingdom, and myself of course, will choose the group who will be our champions. We should achieve this by tomorrow morning and the team should be in pursuit of the thieves by tomorrow afternoon. If anyone here today thinks that they should be included in our party, or have any special skills which would be useful in helping us with our quest, then please make yourselves known to my General Factotum at the marquee.

"May I now take this opportunity to thank you all for attending Our Great Gathering, and I hope that the next time I address you I will be able to tell you of the success of our mission." Her Imperial Majesty, Tallulah the Fairy Queen, turned and with her General Factotum, left the platform and returned to the royal marquee.

The Great Gathering began to break up as some began to head back to their homes in all parts of the Little Kingdom. Most of them were in sombre mood as they digested the news of the calamity that had occurred. A long queue had formed outside the marquee as a mixture of elves, fairies, goblins, nymphs and leprechauns waited to offer their services in the hunt for the villains. It would take some little time before the team would be selected.

PART II
THE QUEST

The specialist team selected by Her Majesty, her General Factotum and the leading citizens of the kingdom was announced at dawn the next day. A list was pinned to a board which was placed at the bottom of the steps to the stage. The team was as follows:

Team Leader: Egbert, the Birkenhead fairy

Fairy Nuff, the Queen's Chief of Security

Fairy Godmother, in charge of magic spells and potions

Two nymphs, Nora and Nancy, for reconnaissance

Two leprechauns, Shaun de Lear and Rick O'Shea, providing some muscle with Gerald the Gorgeous Goblin and his very large trained spider, Syd to provide specialist back up.

The team headed off carrying their light weight packs and equipment shortly after noon, as promised by Queen Tallulah, and by nightfall were far into the Great Forest. They made camp as soon as it began to get dark. None of them had much in the way of sleep the previous night, for obvious reasons, and were keen to get some rest and set off refreshed the next morning. The night was fairly warm and to save time the Fairy Godmother, with the aid or her now repaired magic wand, conjured up a superb hot meal for everyone and there were even some nice fresh flies for Syd the spider. And so everyone retired early to bed for a well earned rest.

At sunrise, following a consultation between the team members, a decision was taken to send the two nymphs, Norah and Nancy, on a reconnaissance flight to try to pick up the trail of the thieves. They returned after about half an hour having gone to the far side of the Great Forest without seeing any trace of them. Then it was the Fairy

Godmother's turn. She just couldn't wait to get started. This was her big moment, the moment she was born for. She knelt before a large flat stone in the middle of the clearing, whilst the others sat around the other side of it facing her. From her large black velvet bag, decorated with silver and gold stars, and crescent moons, she took a red satin cloth which she spread over the stone with a great flourish. This was followed by a black carved object about six inches square and four inches high, with a concave top. This again was placed theatrically in the centre of the red satin cloth. The rest of the team, including Syd the spider, were watching with rapt attention by this time. No-one even blinked. Next from her bag she produced a smaller bag, in blue velvet this time, which seemed to contain something quite heavy.

At this time in proceedings Shaun and Rick, the leprechauns, burst into loud applause thinking that they had just witnessed a conjuring trick, much to the annoyance of the Fairy Godmother, who had been building up to her big moment. Egbert and Fairy Nuff barely managed to suppress a snigger, whilst Gerald the Gorgeous Goblin fell over backwards as Syd the spider ran up the leg of his trousers to hide from the wrath of the Fairy Godmother. The two nymphs, Nora and Nancy, were chortling so much that they almost fell off the tree branch that they were sitting on.

The Fairy Godmother, the wart on the end of her long nose now a bright crimson, struggled to contain her rage. It would be ever so easy to turn them all into stone, or something, and she was sorely tempted. However, she took several deep breaths and settled for giving each individual a glare that made it quite clear that she would brook no more interruptions. She proceeded to untie the cord from the blue velvet bag, and reaching her hand inside, slowly withdrew a large crystal ball. Her small audience looked on in awe. All of them had heard of the crystal ball in their folklore, but none of them had ever seen it. She had her audience back again. Taking the crystal ball reverently in both hands, she placed it ever so carefully in the hollow of the black carved base in the centre. Her audience sat entranced awaiting her next move.

She took a black velvet cloth from her pocket and covered the crystal ball. Then, taking her magic wand, waved it three times over the top in a circular motion and put the wand away. She then removed the cloth from the crystal ball and her audience gazed in silent wonder at the beautiful colours emanating from it. The colours quickly faded, to be replaced by a grey mist swirling around inside the sphere. The Fairy Godmother whispered a few words which sounded like some sort of incantation and the mist began to clear, to be replaced by pictures of forests and meadows. The scenes altered rapidly within the ball, from hill to meadow, from mountain to valley, from the great waters in the west to sheer white walls in the south. She was not amused when what she sought was not to be found. She muttered another incantation, showing signs of her impatience and banged her hands sharply together as her audience watched in silence, afraid even to make the slightest noise. The ball clouded over but quickly cleared. This time the scene changed and appeared to show a clearing on the edge of the Great Forest. Only the Fairy Godmother could see what was in the picture, but she suddenly clapped her hands in delight and excitement at what she saw there. The watching team members realised there had been a significant development and waited for her to tell them about it. She recited another incantation and the crystal ball filled again with the grey mist followed by a display of all the colours of the rainbow, before becoming clear again. Without saying a word she began to return the crystal ball and the other articles to their respective bags, in the reverse order of assembly, and only when she was finished did she speak.

"Eureka," she shouted, "we have found them." The other team members excitedly gathered around her, all of them asking questions at the same time. She held up her hands for silence and only when they were quiet did she continue.

"They are in a clearing at the edge of the Great Forest, no more than a day's march from here. I obviously overestimated them because when I first searched for them with my crystal ball, I was looking too far away. It was when I searched closer to home that I found them. These are the ones who have stolen our crock of gold, ladies and gentleman. It must be returned to its rightful owners."

Egbert the Birkenhead Fairy raised his hand.

"Yes, Egbert?" asked the Fairy Godmother.

"Who are these villains, and do you know how many of them there are, Fairy Godmother?" Egbert asked quietly. The others waited for the reply.

"They are trolls from the far off lands to the north. There are about ten of them and they have a large, four wheeled cart, which has something big in it which is covered over with grass mats. I suspect that this is the crock of gold."

Fairy Nuff now raised his hand and the Fairy Godmother nodded for him to speak.

"We should be able to deal with ten trolls, Fairy Godmother; after all they're hardly the sharpest knives in the box. They are big and strong but that's about it. We will definitely be able to get our property back without too much trouble." The other members of the team murmured agreement.

The Fairy Godmother raised her hands again for silence.

"There is one problem unfortunately," she began. "Their leader is the master villain, Ikabod the Obnoxious."

The other team members gasped in horror as this piece of information sank in.

"I can see that you have all heard of him. He is the epitome of evil, the scourge of all things nice. I pride myself in using magic for good, but he only uses his to destroy."

Egbert raised his hand again, and the Fairy Godmother nodded her assent.

"Can you out magic him if it comes to a head to head, Fairy Godmother?" She thought for a moment and then said,

"We have had our clashes in the past but whilst he has increased his powers as he has grown older, I feel that because of my great age, mine have probably weakened. So in a straight fight he would probably defeat me."

The team groaned at this bad news.

"However," she continued, "that would be in a straight fight. My advantage lies not in my strength but in my much greater experience."

The team brightened up perceptibly at this bit of news. At this, Shaun and Rick, the two leprechauns, glanced quickly at each other, stood up and walked over to the Fairy Godmother, one standing protectively on each side of her.

"He'll have to get past us, Your Majesty," Shaun said.

"And that goes for me as well, Missus," added Rick.

The Fairy Godmother looked a little puzzled for a second, before putting a hand on each of their shoulders and giving them a squeeze.

"I could not wish for better companions than those of you who are with me now," she said. Shaun and Rick blushed deep scarlet as she continued, "We must overcome this evil being for the good of, not only our own people, but for the giants. So, we must now make our plans to recover our property that has been stolen from us, and return it to its rightful place at the end of the rainbow."

The team members voiced their agreement and even Syd the spider, now sitting on Gerald's head, waved his hairy legs in agreement.

Fairy Nuff and Egbert now began, with the help of the Fairy Godmother and other members of the team, to determine a plan of action. It was therefore decided that firstly they would have to catch up with Ikabod the Obnoxious and his gang, and improvise from there.

It was now mid morning and the team set off on a forced march, determined to get as close to the thieves as possible before nightfall.

"We must be aware," the Fairy Godmother told them, "that Ikabod, if he suspects that he is being pursued, is capable of overlooking us and also will know if he is being overlooked, so we must do nothing to warn him of our presence. As we get closer to him we must be increasingly cautious. Do you all understand?" The team nodded solemnly.

They made surprisingly good progress on their march, and just before dusk the nymphs, Norah and Nancy were dispatched, ordered to display all caution, and to see if the villains were still in the area. They returned within half an hour of the dandelion clock, out of breath, but excited to report that they, from the midst of a leafy thicket, had counted ten figures, wrapped in warm sheepskins, asleep on the ground. They had also seen the wagon with the big object in it, wrapped in a cover. They had a cold meal, provided by the magic wand of the Fairy Godmother, and lay down to rest in preparation for the events of the day ahead. Not that any of them felt much like sleep.

Next morning dawned bright and clear and they all rose early, working the stiffness out of their joints. They spoke in whispers although the chances of their being overheard were minimal. After a quick breakfast they moved off towards the thieves campsite During the team's conversations the previous evening, Fairy Nuff had raised the question of why the thieves had decided to camp for such a long time at this particular spot. They must have known that there would be pursuit of some kind, so why hang around. Various suggestions had been put forward, for example, perhaps they thought that the theft had not yet been discovered or perhaps they thought that their trail had not yet been picked up. Anyway it was decided that the team would close in on their camp and remain concealed until it was time to move in.

Gerald and Syd the spider, along with Fairy Nuff, would circle around to the left side of the camp. Shaun and Rick, the two leprechauns, together with Egbert the Birkenhead Fairy, were to circle around to the right. The Fairy Godmother would approach from the front for a head on confrontation with her old adversary, Ikabod. Her reasoning being that if any of the other team members came against him they would have very little chance of survival. On the other hand they would be able to deal adequately with the trolls. The team grudgingly agreed that she was probably right on that assumption. It was also agreed that the two nymphs, Norah and Nancy, should not get too close to the enemy, but simply observe how things would turn out. In the event that the villains were victorious, then they should head back and report to Queen Tallulah as soon as possible.

And so the die was cast. At a signal from the Fairy Godmother the groups silently set off to take up their positions.

The Fairy Godmother moved slowly and carefully through the long grass, pausing to listen from time to time. All was quiet. Too quiet! She could, by using her magic have overlooked the camp, but as she had explained to the others, Ikabod would have become aware of her presence very quickly. She moved forward a little more and suddenly felt dizzy. She stopped for a moment turning her head from side to side to try to clear the feeling. Then she knew what it was without a doubt. She was being overlooked. The evil one had found her. She walked a little further and found that she was out of the long grass and into the clearing. She was directly in front of the camp site about thirty metres away from the wagon. Facing her and looking more evil and even uglier than the last time she had laid eyes on him, stood Ikabod the Obnoxious. Behind him, standing in a little row, were the other nine trolls, smirking menacingly. Ikabod took a few steps towards the Fairy Godmother and stopped a sadistic grin on his nasty face.

"Fairy Godmother! How very nice to see you again. I must say you are very brave to come here like this. I knew of course that if anyone came after us it would be you and I am very glad that you did. I have an old score to settle with you, some unfinished business, if you like. By the way, I also know that you have not come alone. My friends here will take care of your little band of helpers whilst I finish my business with you, forever!"

The Fairy Godmother stood silently and totally relaxed, listening to Ikabod. Her brain was working frantically, trying to find a way out of her predicament. Ikabod took her silence for fear and his little chest puffed up. He started to strut up and down as he spoke,

"You have been a thorn in my side for a long time, old woman, and I intend to rid myself of you forever."

"A question first, ugly one," the Fairy Godmother finally said.

Ikabod flinched as though struck across the face, "ask away old woman," he snarled. "You haven't much time left to talk."

"Why did you steal the Crock of Gold and how did you know where to find it?" she asked.

"What a stupid question you old crone! Don't you know that whoever has *that* Crock of Gold has the world in his hands? The Giants will do anything to get their economy back on its feet again. You do-gooders used to feed the gold into the economic system secretly, and they not knowing that, congratulated themselves on turning things around by good business sense. I will not do things that way. They will know that it is me saving their skins and I will claim my reward for my services." As he spoke his voice rose in pitch and he strutted up and down, faster and faster, his little hands clasped behind his back.

"What will be your reward, oh great one?" the Fairy Godmother asked sarcastically. The sarcasm was totally lost on Ikabod.

"Reward! Reward!" he shouted, "My reward will be the whole world. I shall rule it. What do you think of that, old woman?"

The Fairy Godmother looked him straight in the eye and said slowly and deliberately,

"Not while I'm still here you little toad. I'm sorry, I withdraw that. It would be an insult to toads."

Ikabod cackled manically and said, "You won't be here for much longer, old woman."

"Okay then, how did you know where the Crock of Gold was buried?" she asked. "Its hiding place was known to only a chosen few."

The troll looked at her scornfully.

"It was easy. I watched when they went to get some gold to pass on to the Giants. When they went away I went back with my friends here and dug it up. It was so easy. I'm surprised that no-one had done it before."

"The thought of stealing anything in our land would never enter the mind of our poorest citizen. It would have to be a low life like you to come up with an idea like that."

"Compliments will get you nowhere, old woman. Now we have talked enough. It's time for you to go, I'm tired of this badinage." He raised his right hand to point at the Fairy Godmother and shouted, "Goodbye, old woman, forever!"

A bolt of blue light flashed from his hand towards the Fairy Godmother, who had been expecting such a move. She plucked her magic wand from her sleeve and parried his attack with a bolt of her own. The two surges of electrical energy crashed together, crackling and spitting. The rest of the trolls shot off at high speed at this turn of events and took refuge in a little clump of pine trees at the edge of the clearing. Ikabod scowled after them and muttered something about not being able to get the staff. He then turned to face the Fairy Godmother.

"I don't need any help to deal with you anyway, old woman. Have some of that!" and he launched another bolt of blue lightning at his hated adversary. The Fairy Godmother launched a bolt of her own which deflected the troll's. He was getting very annoyed by the ability of the old woman as he called her to not only parry his electrical thrusts, but to hit back using some of his own medicine. He comforted himself with the knowledge of these thrusts and parries, a little like fencing really, used lots of energy. He was younger and stronger than the old bat! There was only going to be one winner. Buoyed by this knowledge he launched into a series of thrusts at the Fairy Godmother. She in turn parried every bolt that was aimed at her, the air in the clearing crackling with the bursts of electrical energy. The smell of ozone was heavy in the clear morning air. She knew that she was using up all her strength. How many more parries would she manage? The troll sensed that she was weakening and launched another series of attacks, each stronger than before, the crash and crackle of the discharges now almost deafening. The Fairy Godmother now staggering under the onslaught, and realising that the end was now near, totally missed her block on one of his bolts, which luckily was off target anyway. Her bolt of lightning struck a huge oak tree about twenty feet from Ikabod, blasting great lumps of the tree into the air. The Fairy Godmother dropped her arms. She ached all over and, totally exhausted, slowly sank to her knees. She had done her best, now there was nothing left.

Ikabod looked around at the damage done to the big oak tree and cackled with glee. "A bit off target there old woman, wouldn't you say? Do you want to plead for your life and those of your misguided companions? Eh? Eh? Of course you know that it will be to no avail, don't you? Well goodbye! I can't say that it has been a pleasure, other than this bit where I dispatch you to wherever Fairy Godmothers go."

He began to raise his arm to fire another and probably the last bolt at the helpless Fairy Godmother, when the air was filled with the sound of splintering timber. The troll turned at the sound just in time to see the huge oak, weighing many tons, falling towards him. He screamed in fear and fired the bolt at the tree. He was just a little bit late and as the huge tree fell on him, his bolt of electrical energy caused the tree to glow red hot, then white hot, and as it crashed down on the evil troll it turned into a pile of grey ash. If Ikabod had been able to look at the Fairy Godmother before the tree crashed down on top of him, he would have seen a smile of triumph on her face.

The rest of the team, with the exception of Gerald and Syd the spider, appeared from their hiding places and ran to the Fairy Godmother's aid. Egbert, Fairy Nuff, Shaun and Rick and the two nymphs, Norah and Nancy, crowded around her, laughing and crying at the same time with relief and joy at her victory over the evil one.

"Where are Gerald and Syd?" she asked, "and where have those trolls gone? Have they escaped?"

The answer to both these questions became obvious a moment later, when into the clearing walked the trolls, each of them cocooned from head to waist in a sticky spider's web, courtesy of a very proud Syd, now sitting on Gerald's shoulder, both of them looking pleased with themselves.

Good had prevailed over evil.

PART III
THE RETURN

It was still only noon and the Fairy Godmother, though still tired after her battle with Ikabod, decided that they should head back to their homeland as soon as possible. She provided a meal for everyone, including the trolls, and prepared to leave. First of all she dispatched the two nymphs to return to Queen Tallulah with the good news of their success, and to expect the arrival of the team, the Crock of Gold and their prisoners, in three days time.

After the trolls had been harnessed to the shafts, all the members of the team all climbed up onto the wagon which carried the Crock of Gold, made themselves comfortable on the sheepskins belonging to the trolls and so the journey home began. The trail through the Great Forest was narrow and twisting, but such was the strength of the trolls that they made excellent time. The weather was warm and sunny during the day and mild at night, so with frequent stops for food and rest, the journey went amazingly well. The Fairy Godmother was now fully recovered from her exertions. The trolls were no trouble at all. It seemed that they were being treated much better than they had been by their ex-master, Ikabod. As for the other team members, they were in high spirits now that they were going home.

And so it was, with the sun at its zenith on the third day of their journey, the little band passed from the forest and into the lush meadows of the Great Glade. They came to a sudden halt as their ears were assaulted by the thunderous cheers of thousands of little people from all over the kingdom. The trolls were terrified that they were going to be killed, but the team members managed to calm them down. As the wagon began to move forward again the huge crowd parted and the team could see in the distance, at the head of the Great Glade, the huge marquee with the stage at the front and the royal standard of her Imperial Majesty, Queen Tallulah, the Fairy Queen, flying proudly from its flag pole.

It took the team almost an hour to reach the Queen's marquee as everyone in the crowd wanted to shake their hands. The wagon was almost full of flower petals that had been thrown by the jubilant crowd. At last the wagon halted in front of the platform. Queen Tallulah sat on a golden throne, a beaming smile of pleasure on her face as she waited to receive her champions. Her Majesty's General Factotum, now wearing a new purple jacket with gold braid and sporting a brand new pair of wellies, stepped forward and helped each member of the team to step safely from the wagon onto the platform.

The first was Gerald with Syd sitting on his right shoulder. Next were Shaun de Lear and Rick O'Shea. The two nymphs, Nancy and Nora, were already on the platform having arrived much earlier than the rest of the team. Then came Fairy Nuff followed by Egbert the Birkenhead fairy. As each of them stepped onto the platform they were greeted by rapturous applause from the ecstatic multitude, but what they had received was exceeded tenfold when the Fairy Godmother was helped on to the platform. The wagon still pulled by the nine trolls and containing the Crock of Gold, was taken away to a place of safety by a troop of her Majesty's Guards. The Queen congratulated each and every one of the team personally and only then did she address the huge crowd who applauded wildly. It took the General Factotum several minutes to quieten the crowd. In fact it was only when he threatened to get the Great Battle Horn player to give a recital that the crowd became silent.

She began, "People of the Great Glade we have gathered here again this morning to witness the return of our stolen property; property that for eons, we have used as a force for good and for the benefit of all creatures, both in our world and the world of the Giants. The people who stole our property did so to further their own greed and their thirst for power. Thankfully we had a team of people who were more than a match for the evil ones. So as a token of thanks not only from us here today and no doubt from the Land of the Giants as well, every member of our recovery team will become an Honoured Knight of our Realm, including Syd the spider, by the way." (If Syd could have blushed he would have done.) This was greeted by thunderous applause.

"We shall begin to feed in some of our recovered wealth into the economy of the Giants quite soon and things should return to normal. As we have said before, good will always triumph over evil. So, to finish off, I declare a week of public holidays. In the mean time food and drink will be provided for everyone in the Great Glade today. I am sure that there will be entertainment to be enjoyed by everyone. Thank you all." Her Imperial Majesty, Tallulah the Fairy Queen walked back to her marquee smiling broadly, to the deafening applause of her loyal subjects.

Her place on the platform was taken by her General Factotum and he called the gathering to order again and again and again until he was almost hoarse. Eventually the crowd, impressed with his resilience finally quietened down, at least enough for him to be heard.

"Ladies and Gentleman," he began, "Her Majesty has asked me to inform you of some of the attractions that have been arranged for your enjoyment and pleasure today. The venues for these are sited throughout the Great Glade. First on our list is a talk by one of our leprechauns, Donny Gall, on 'How to Avoid Buying a Pig in a Poke.' Next we have 'Haggis Juggling for the over eighties' by Aberdeen Angus. At the far end of the Great Glade the well known entrepreneur Basil Ponsonby Smallpiece will be giving a demonstration on 'The Art of String Vest Manufacture for Beginners' (and what to do with them when you've made them). Whilst at this end of the Great Glade there will be a demonstration of 'One handed Knitting and Crocheting for Retired Gentlemen of a Certain Age'. Other attractions this afternoon include Pig Racing, with a demonstration by our old friend Cecil the Warthog, now fully recovered from his coming together with a tree. The well known and very popular Muffin Throwing Championships will also be held this afternoon. Will all muffins taking part please report to the organiser as soon as possible. Last but not least, our Great Battle Horn player, Herr Port, will give a recital of Brahms piano concerto on the bagpipes for your delectation. So, let the festivities begin." With a sweeping bow to the cheering throng the General Factotum left the platform.

Things had certainly returned to normal in the Kingdom of Tallulah, Queen of the Fairies and hopefully very soon to the Land of the Giants.

THE END

A Seat In The Gods

Peter began to run. The rain that had been spitting gently a short time ago was now torrential, a typical English summer thunderstorm.

He'd had a torrid Monday morning at work. After a weekend, during which he and his wife Betty had totally relaxed, Peter found it hard to get back into work mode. On top of that a couple of key members of staff had called in sick with flu symptoms, and a newly installed computer system had been giving problems. Peter struggled on manfully to keep his head above water, and in the brief moments when he had time, he glanced out of the office window and could see that it was a pleasant, sunny day outside. He decided that busy or not he was going to enjoy his lunch break. A sandwich and a seat in the sunshine by the river was definitely on the cards.

Lunch time arrived and typically, after having been an absolutely lovely morning, as soon as Peter had appeared outside the building on his way to lunch, the heavens had opened. He was in his shirt sleeves, like most of the people on their way to lunch, all of them now scurrying everywhere trying to find shelter from the downpour, as a flash of lightning and a crash of thunder spurred them on. Almost all the shop doorways were crowded to capacity and beyond and so he raced round a corner into a little narrow side street. He had no recollection of ever having been in the street before, and to his surprise, saw a large opening in a shop front. The large wooden doors had been pulled apart to provide access to a room, filled with old furniture and bric-a-brac. There were about twenty people inside the gloomy interior, most of them seemingly like himself, just sheltering from the rain. Peter stood at the back of the little crowd, most of whom were chatting amongst themselves, and discussing the anomalies of the British weather. Suddenly someone began banging a gavel, and a loud voice said,

"Ladies and gentlemen, please! Can we get on with the rest of the sale? We only have a few more items to auction and then we can all go home." Someone whispered under their breath that if the rain would go off they would go home now. Peter looked up to see where the banging of the gavel and the loud voice had come from, and eventually spotted a little man standing behind a dias at the far end of the room. He wore a black suit with waistcoat and a snow white shirt with a winged collar and a grey tie. He had on a pair of pince-nez and apart from a little fringe of hair around the back and sides of his head, was completely bald. His voice though, was strong and resonant and his diction clear and precise. A large hand-painted sign on the wall above and behind him declared that Simpson, Devlin and Makepiece were indeed Auctioneers, Valuers and Estate Agents and that auctions of fine furniture were held every Monday and Thursday mornings at 11.00 o'clock. Peter thought to himself that the Monday sale was fortunate indeed, otherwise he and some of the others assembled in the room would be even wetter than they were at present. He glanced over his shoulder to see if the rain had eased enough for him to slip out of the door before the auction continued, but alas the rain if anything was heavier than ever, the splashes of the large drops in the puddles on the pavement were punctuated by lightning and the crash of thunder. The little street outside the auctioneer's was now quite dark and someone switched on the inside lights in the sale room. This did not help very much as the globes covering the bulbs seemed to be quite dusty and they were only about sixty watts. He glanced at his watch and was annoyed to see that fifteen minutes of his lunch break had already gone and still the rain lashed down. He decided to stay a little longer and hope that it would go off.

The assembled crowd had started to talk amongst themselves again and the murmur of conversation was rising. The gavel crashed down again on its block on the dias, startling the talkers into silence.

"Ladies and gentlemen, we come to lot number one hundred and nine, a 1930s hallstand and mirror. Do I hear twenty pounds to start the bidding?" He gazed around the assembled faces. Nothing.

"Do I hear ten pounds?" Again he looked expectantly around them all. Most people avoided his eyes, feet shuffled on the concrete floor. Most of them would have headed out of the door had the rain gone off.

"Come on now ladies and gentlemen, do I hear five pounds?" A little old lady in the front row finally cracked under thre pressure of the auctioneer's piercing gaze, and seemingly did little more than blink. It was enough and the auctioneer, asking quickly on any advance on five pounds, and of course receiving no further bids, quickly banged down his gavel to complete the sale.

Several other small lots went for minimal amounts of money to people who purchased them rather than be cast out into the elements, (the rain was still pouring down outside.) The auctioneer, Peter could not decide whether he was Mr Simpson, Mr Devlin or Mr Makepiece, not that it made much difference, finally said,

"Ladies and gentleman, our last lot of the sale is a pair of red, upholstered, theatre seats dating to the mid 1920s. Can I have a bid to start me off please?" His eyes wandered over the fidgeting assembly,

"Come along now ladies and gentlemen, make me an offer." Everyone found something that really had to be done. Handkerchiefs were produced, noses blown, loose change was counted, the contents of wallets and handbags were examined as if the owner's life depended on it.

"Do I hear ten pounds for two beautiful theatre seats? Just the job for when visitors arrive, or for you and your husband or wife to bring back the memories of your courting days in the back row of the Odeon!" Someone in the crowd laughed dutifully.

He glanced over the little crowd again and as his eyes met Peter's, an old chap who was standing slightly to one side of Peter, turned quickly to look out of the door to see if the rain had gone off. Unfortunately as he turned, his large shopping basket full of whatever it was full of, collided with a very tender part of Peter's anatomy. He immediately raised his hand as if to fend off the old gentleman and the auctioneer, quick as a flash said,

"Ten pounds bid, any advance on ten pounds? Going, going, gone!" His gavel crashed down and Peter being rendered hors de combat was unable to explain to the auctioneer what had happened. The auctioneer's assistant now appeared at Peter's elbow and said,

"That'll be £10 sir. A lovely pair of old seats. Would you like them delivered or will you take them with you?" Peter now recovered sufficiently to be able to speak, decided not to make a fuss. He handed over a ten pound note and gave his address for the delivery of the seats, wondering at the same time how he was going to explain all this to Betty. He glanced around the auction room and discovered that everyone, including the auctioneer and helper had gone, and when he looked through the door he saw that the sun was once more shining and the pavement was drying. He looked again at his watch and noticed that he still had forty minutes of his lunch break left.

The seats were delivered to Peter's house the next day. Fortunately for him, his wife Betty had a fine sense of humour and had laughed heartily when she had heard the story of his purchase. She was quite amazed when Peter told her how old they were, and even he was pleasantly surprised when he saw the excellent condition that they were in. The dark wooden frames were highly polished and the plush, dark red upholstery on the tip up seats appeared to be almost new. On the back of each of the seats was a little brass plate, one stamped number twenty five and the other number twenty six. The little plates sparkled brightly.

Peter and Betty over their thirty years of marriage had collected the odd antique that they had liked and their little bungalow, on the outskirts of Harrogate, had quite a few old pieces of furniture dotted about within its rooms. Betty decided that as they were theatre seats, and in such fine condition, she would have them fitted in the lounge, where they had just installed one of the new wide screen television sets, complete with wrap round sound.

"We can sit on them and watch our new television, and during the commercials I can bring round the pop corn and ice creams." She giggled at the thought and Peter gave her a hug.

"You'll need a torch and have to show me to my seat," he said, and they both fell around laughing.

Peter rearranged the lounge furniture and the seats were duly installed to Betty's satisfaction. Both of them had to admit that they looked very nice sitting against the wall opposite the new TV. They were quite busy over the next few evenings and it was Saturday when Betty suggested that after tea they could go into the lounge and watch their television from their newly acquired seats.

Betty and Peter duly retired to the lounge after the dishes had been washed and tidied away. He placed a little coffee table in front of the old theatre seats and poured a drink for Betty and himself. They sat down and switched on the TV, marvelling at the quality of the picture on the new wide screen, and the sound that seemed to come from all around them. It was like being in the middle of the audience. Their old television set had left a lot to be desired performance wise. Betty had kept on at Peter for some time to buy a new one, until he finally succumbed. He had opted, or they had opted, for one of the new wide screen jobs, with multiple speakers. As they relaxed on the old theatre seats, which were 'ever so comfortable', they really felt it was money well spent.

They had initially intended to watch the lottery and they were quite pleased to find that they had won £10. This was followed by a Clint Eastwood movie and as they were both fans of his, they enjoyed this as well. During the course of the evening Peter topped up their drinks and they were in a very happy state of mind later on when they found themselves watching an old style Music Hall. It was something after the style of the Good Old Days, (which they both loved,) complete with compere who used very long words, much to the amusement of not only Peter and Betty, but the audience as well.

As they watched acts such as Jean Hardy's Ten Regent Kids, described as Variety's cleverest children; Jack Henry, comedian; Thom and Mac - comedy acrobats and Madame Della's Dogs – the Acme of Animal Training the compere had called them, they found themselves applauding with the audience at the end of each act and they sat enthralled as the show went on. They were quite put out when the curtain came down and the show ended. It had been quite a long day and they must have dozed off together, as they sometimes did, and Betty woke with a start to find a French film with English subtitles on the television, and discovered that it was ten minutes past two in the morning. She woke Peter and after switching off the TV and lights they went to bed.

Next morning, probably because of their late night, they got up later than usual, and over breakfast they talked about the show they had watched the night before. They had both thoroughly enjoyed it and thought it such a refreshing change from the usual dross that they were subjected to at weekends. Peter thought that the costumes were fabulous, not only the acts but the audience as well, and he was determined to watch the programme next time it was on.

Betty and Peter normally only used the lounge at weekends or when visitors arrived, and usually sat in the living room after tea in a couple of old comfortable armchairs, reading or listening to the radio or CDs. It was the following Saturday night before they retired to the lounge again. Peter poured them each a drink and they settled down in their new seats to watch the lottery. This time they didn't have any luck, and watched the Terminator starring Arnold Swartzenegger. They had both seen the picture before but enjoyed it again on their new equipment. Peter acting as barman, dispensed their refreshments, when suddenly on came the old Music Hall with the elegantly dressed compere and his wonderful long winded introductions of the acts, the audience oohing and aahing good naturedly at his hilarious descriptions. They were treated to a feast of acts that Peter and Betty had never heard of before such as Miriam Morrison, a 'noted' soprano; Herbert Short a tenor/comedian; Olga Ashford a speciality dancer, and the Imperial Cabaret Girls. They both agreed it was wonderful that there was so much new talent getting their chance on TV. Once more they thoroughly enjoyed the show, and again were quite sad when the curtain came down. This time it was Peter who woke with a start to find it was one thirty in the morning and the late night movie was being shown. He woke Betty and they went off to bed.

They were quite bleary eyed next morning, but both of them chatted nonstop about the show that they had seen the evening before. Both of them agreed it was the best thing either of them had seen on television for yonks!

On Monday evening Peter arrived home from work and came through to the dining room where Betty was laying the table in preparation for the dinner. Peter gave her a kiss on the cheek and asked her if she'd had a good day. Betty replied that she had been quite busy with her household chores.

"Oh, I nearly forgot. I asked both Margaret and Sally if they had been watching the Old Time Music Hall on television on Saturday evenings recently, but neither of them had seen it." Margaret and Sally were two of Betty's best friends.

"Funny you should say that," said Peter, "I asked some of the chaps at work, but they haven't seen it either. George who works in the office reckons that we must have been getting some freak reception or perhaps the tuning on our new television might be out a little bit. George is a bit of an expert on things like that. He recommended that we get the people who installed our new TV to come and check it out. I rang them this afternoon and they'll come and have a look at it tomorrow morning.

The next evening Peter came home from work and over the evening meal Betty told Peter about the engineer's visit.

"He checked absolutely everything," said Betty, "even the aerial, and everything is spot on. He can find nothing wrong whatsoever. The only thing that he could come up with was that sunspots had perhaps caused a freak reception. There had been reports that people in different parts of the country had been picking up foreign programmes on their televisions, occasionally."

"Well that's probably what it is then," Peter replied, "George did suggest that as well. Anyway, it's not as if it was a bad programme. Let's hope we get some more of it."

Peter wandered through to the lounge after supper and poured himself a drink. He switched on the television and turned to sit on one of the old seats. He stopped and called to Betty to come into the lounge. Betty arrived looking startled.

"What's wrong love?" she asked looking at Peter.

"Nothing really, but I just thought that these old seats looked absolutely lovely. What a good job you've made of them." Betty flushed with pleasure.

"I haven't really done anything to them other than brush the fabric and polish the wooden bits, but you're right, they look as good as new. When we got them," continued Betty, "I noticed a scorch mark, probably from a cigarette end on one of them, but I can't find it now."

"Oh well," said Peter, "it shows how good a job you've made of them."

They sat down on the old seats and Peter poured Betty a drink and they watched television for half an hour then went off to bed.

Saturday night arrived and after tea Peter and Betty went through to watch their usual programmes. Sometime later they found themselves again watching the old time Music Hall. Neither of them could remember the programme starting, but the compere was again in really fine form, and the audience clapped and cheered as he introduced the acts. Peter and Betty sat enthralled, unable to take their eyes off the stage. Hetty King, Chas Austin as the little old lady; Lilly Morris a comedienne; Arthur Prince and Jim; Talbot O'Farrell, an Irish entertainer; Frank, Mary and Iris who were jugglers. They were absolutely superb.

Neither Peter nor Betty remembered the show ending. They woke about half past one and headed upstairs to bed.

Next morning at breakfast, Peter and Betty could again talk of nothing but the acts that they had enjoyed the night before.

"We must have had some more freak reception," said Peter, "but you know, all of this has only started since we got those old theatre seats and also on a Saturday."

"Yes," said Betty, "but we also got our new TV around the same time."

"You're right," Peter replied, "it's probably freak reception like the man said. However I'd like to know a little more about those seats, where they came from, who owned them for example? I think I'll pop down to the auctioneer's on Monday during my lunch break and see if I can find out anything about them."

On Monday Peter remembered that it was auction day at the sale room, so decided against going down to Simpson, Devlin and Makepiece to try to get some information about the seats. He remembered what had happened on his last visit! Not wanting to inadvertently purchase something else, he postponed his visit until Tuesday lunchtime.

He arrived to find the large wooden sliding doors, the entrance to the sale room, tightly closed. He had a moment of panic when he thought that the premises were closed up for the day. Then he noticed another door, close to where he stood, which had a glass panel, in the centre of which hung a dusty, faded sign which said OPEN. He could see through the glass that there was a light on inside, so he tried the door handle and the door swung inwards. At the same time a bell attached to the door clanged loudly. He stepped inside and closed the door, the bell ringing yet again.

He was standing in the sale room and although there was a light on, it did not do much to penetrate the gloom. Peter looked around the room noting the items of furniture and other pieces which filled the sales area to capacity. He tried to spot an office or even a door to one, but because of the gloom was unable to do so. Then he saw the old oak dais against one wall and decided to try to make his way over to that, reasoning that it might be close to where someone might be found. He was halfway there, carefully picking his way through the sales items, when a disembodied voice stopped him dead in his tracks.

"Good afternoon sir. Is there anything in particular that you would like to see?"

The voice was vaguely familiar and Peter peered around trying to see where it was coming from. Out of the gloom emerged the diminutive figure of the auctioneer who had been conducting the sale on the day that Peter had purchased the seats.

"Oh hello," he said to the little man, "I'm sorry to trouble you. I'm not really looking for anything at the moment except some information on something I purchased here three or four weeks ago."

"What was the article sir, and how can I be of service?"

"Well," said Peter, "it was a pair of old theatre seats, and I was wondering if you could tell me where they came from?"

The auctioneer thought for a moment and said,

"Come into the office for a moment and I'll see what I can do." He led the way to a wooden door which was covered by a dark curtain, behind the dais, and Peter followed him into a brightly lit modern office, complete with computers, printers and fax machines. Two young ladies were busy typing invoices. Both looked up and smiled as the two men entered. Peter's face was a picture and the little man grinned at his expression of amazement. He held out his hand and hesitantly Peter took it. The little man's grip was firm and dry.

"I'm Alec Simpson," he said, I'm the senior partner in Devlin, Simpson and Makepiece. You look a little perturbed Mr?...."

"Oh, I'm sorry," said Peter, "let me introduce myself. I'm Peter Matthews. I apologise for gawping, but this office is such a contrast to the room outside."

"Well," replied Mr Simpson, "out there is part of the image. It's what the people expect to see when they go to an auction. If we cleaned all the furniture up and installed fluorescent lighting and carpet on the floor, it would spoil the effect. People like to feel they've discovered an antique or got a bargain at the right price, and the atmosphere in our sale room helps with that illusion. What is not an illusion is that this is a very good business. We scour the country for old furniture and household effects, and such is our turnover that this modern office with it's computers and other such equipment is necessary to help us keep on top of our business."

Mr Simpson still wore his black suit with his waistcoat, his snow white shirt with its winged collar and his grey tie. His black shoes gleamed and his fringe of hair around his bald head was neatly trimmed. Peter noticed that behind his rimless spectacles the little man's blue eyes twinkled with amusement.

"Now Peter, may I call you Peter?" Alex Simpson asked.

Peter nodded, "Please do sir."

"What would you like to know? A pair of old theatre seats you said?"

"Yes," replied Peter, "for instance can you tell me who put them up for auction?

"Can you tell me the date they were sold and the lot number?" asked Mr Simpson.

Peter took out his wallet and extracted the bill of sale and handed it to the senior partner. Mr Simpson raised his glasses and peered closely at the paper. He walked across to an unmanned pc and punched a few keys. He watched the screen closely for a minute and then said,

"Yes, I remember those old seats. I said at the time we got them that I didn't think they would make much money as they didn't look all that good. We got them as part of a house clearance. An old gentleman had died and his daughter and her husband had asked us to dispose of the contents of his home. By the time the stuff had come up for auction the old seats didn't look too bad, and as you know the rest is history. Do you have a problem with the seats, Peter?" asked Mr Simpson.

"No," said Peter, "but I would like to know something about their history. It can't be every day that a pair of seats like these come up for auction."

"You're right," said the auctioneer, "however, whilst I do have a contact number for the people who owned the seats, I'm sure you can appreciate I can't pass the number on to you without their consent." Peter nodded his understanding and Mr Simpson continued, "however, if you like I'll contact them later today and give you a ring this evening with their reply." Peter gave Mr Simpson his home telephone number, and thanking him profusely, left the premises and returned to work. The afternoon dragged in and Peter was glad when it was home time.

He brought Betty up to date with his efforts at the auctioneers, and after that they settled down to await the phone call from Mr Simpson.

The phone rang at eight o'clock, and Peter lifted the receiver quickly. It was Alec Simpson.

"Evening Peter," he said, "sorry it took me so long to contact you, I couldn't get through to the owners all afternoon. The good news is that Mr and Mrs Mills are quite happy to hear from you. If you have a pen and paper handy I'll give you their telephone number." Peter wrote down the number and having thanked Mr Simpson again, put down the telephone and immediately dialled the number that he had been given. The phone was answered on the third ring by a lady with a faint Liverpudlian accent.

"Hello, Mrs Mills speaking."

Peter hesitated for a moment before replying.

"Good evening Mrs Mills, it's Peter Matthews, Mr Simpson said it would be OK to give you a ring regarding the old theatre seats."

"Oh yes, Mr Matthews. It's nice to talk to you. How can I help you?"

"I'd like to know a bit more about the old seats, for instance how did you come by them, and do you know which theatre they came from?" asked Peter.

"Well, actually they belonged to my father who was a building contractor when he was younger," said Mrs Mills. "He died about four months ago and my husband and I decided to dispose of the contents of his house and workshop, and that's when the old seats first came to light, and also how the whole job lot arrived at the auctioneers. It was funny really. The seats had been buried under lots of old timber and bits and pieces for some time, but in spite of that, did not appear to be in bad condition. We've also found some of my Dad's old diaries, he kept one every year of his life, and I think I saw at least one reference to the seats in one of them. We also found some of the old playbills from the theatre where the seats came from. He'd had these framed and I'm sure there were four or five of them and we still have them at our house. Would you like to have a look at them?"

Peter agreed readily. "When would it be convenient to come and have a look?" asked Peter.

"Well," said Mrs Mills, "it's Tuesday now, we are away all day Wednesday, how about Thursday about three o'clock?"

Peter hesitated. Could he get away from work? Let's worry about that later, he thought.

"Yes, Mrs Mills, that will be fine. Betty, my wife, and I will be there about three o'clock on Thursday."

Mrs Mills gave Peter an address on the outskirts of Southport, which was about two hours drive from his own home.

Peter and Betty pulled up outside Mrs Mills' house in their old Rover right on three o'clock on Thursday afternoon. It was a beautiful bungalow built in the early fifties, with a very tidy front garden, and a crazy paved path from the gate to the front door. As Peter and Betty approached the gate, the front door opened and a lady of around sixty appeared. She gave them both a warm welcoming smile and ushered them into a long hallway, carpeted in dark blue Wilton. A highly polished, Victorian hall stand stood on one side. She opened a door and showed them into the lounge where Mr Mills, her husband, came forward to greet them. After the introductions Mrs Mills sat them down on a very comfortable leather settee, and leaving them in the company of her husband, went off to make a cup of tea. The living room, like the outside of the bungalow, was beautifully arranged. All the wooden furniture shone and everything was highly polished. Not a speck of dust anywhere.

Mr Mills proved to be quite a nice chap as well, and he chatted amicably to Peter and Betty as they waited for Mrs Mills to return with the tea. This arrived accompanied by some very nice homemade biscuits which were dispatched with some aplomb by the visitors, much to the delight of Mrs Mills. When they had finished, Mr Mills excused himself and left the room, returning some minutes later carrying some framed playbills, and a cardboard box containing some books.

"These are the things we found belonging to Margaret's father," said Mr Mills. "These books are his diaries dating from when he first set up his company in 1941. His first job as a contractor was to demolish the old Palace Theatre on Merseyside, and to clear the site. The theatre had been destroyed by a German bomber during a raid in the early part of 1941. Apparently the aircraft had got lost in bad weather, dumped its bombs the first chance it got, and headed for home. The bombs, instead of landing on the docks, hit a built up area instead. Mrs Mills produced an old yellowed newspaper. The bombing was headlined on the front page. 'TWO KILLED IN GERMAN AIR RAID' stated the headline. The article went on to describe how a German bomber had shed its lethal load on a packed theatre on Merseyside on a Saturday night. The theatre had been badly damaged and set on fire, the amazing thing was that only two people had been killed and twenty three injured, several seriously. The two dead people, a man and a woman who had only been married for two weeks, were named as Philip and Ethel Martin. They had been killed by falling masonry. The fire had been brought under control after several hours and the badly damaged building made safe.

Mr Mills produced a book belonging to his wife's father, which was in fact his diary for the period. Apparently, the building minus most of its roof had been left open to the elements for some months before it was decided to demolish what was left of it. This was when Mrs Mills' father had got the job of clearing the old theatre. He had hired men and equipment and his business had taken off. In his diary he had described going into the building in order to clear out the interior prior to commencing demolition. A lot of the seats had been destroyed and rubble and burnt timbers lay everywhere. The demolition squad had worked for days clearing away the wreckage from inside the building. It was therefore quite a surprise, when amongst the dirt and soot it was found that a pair of seats were in much better condition than the rest, despite the fact that the interior of the theatre had been open to the elements for some considerable time. They were in a quite dry and usable condition. The only ones out of over four hundred seats. According to his diary, Mrs Mills' father had taken them home, meaning to restore them at some time in the future. Among other items that he had salvaged were some old playbills and he had eventually had these framed. These playbills listed the acts appearing at the theatre and were dated about four weeks prior to the bombing.

Peter sat quietly, his face pale as he mentally digested these facts. Betty watched her husband anxiously, knowing that he was deeply troubled by what he had learned. Mrs Mills interrupted Peter's reverie.

"We read through some of Dad's diaries and we found that sometime later, perhaps two or three years after the war, he had installed the seats in his living room. Apparently without too much effort on his part, the seats had returned to almost pristine condition and he and my mother would sit in them and they would listen to the radio. However, I remember him saying that they used to get some strange programmes on their old Bakelite radio, usually on a Saturday night. He hadn't tied these in with the old seats, but apparently they stopped when he put the old seats into the shed. He'd done some checking and discovered that the programmes had usually started a week or two before the anniversary of the bombing."

"What was the actual date of the raid?" asked Peter. Mr Mills answered this question.

"It's the sixtieth anniversary this Saturday night," he said. Peter gripped Betty's hand tightly.

"May I have a look at the old playbills?" he asked.

"Yes of course," said Mrs Mills, glancing uneasily across the room at her husband.

Peter laid the framed playbills out on the floor in chronological order, beginning with the earliest and ending with the one that had been on at the theatre the night of the bombing. He motioned to Betty to kneel on the floor beside him. Mr and Mrs Mills stood silently watching them. Peter pointed out a couple of the acts, namely the Regent Kids; Jack Henry, comedian; and Madame Della's Dogs.

"Do you remember those Betty?" he asked. Betty nodded. He moved to the next and pointed out Miriam Morrison, the noted Soprano; Olga Ashford, dancer; the Imperial Cabaret Girls.

"Those were the next week." He turned to the penultimate one, dated one week before the bombing.

"This was the show that we saw last Saturday night. Do you recognise those names, love?" Betty's face was now as pale as Peter's. She nodded dumbly. Peter ran his finger down the list of acts. Lilly Morris; Arthur, Prince and Jim; Charles Austin as the Little Old Lady; and top of the bill, Hetty King, famous for her male impersonations.

"Don't you see what that means?" he asked, continuing without waiting for anyone to answer.

"That means that the next bill is the last one ever to be shown at the theatre," he said, "after that it was destroyed, and virtually the only things to survive were those two seats which are now sitting in our lounge!"

Mrs Mills looked at Peter and Betty.

"You know, I remember my Dad doing exactly the same thing that you have just done. He didn't really blame the seats for the strange happenings, but he reckoned there was something funny about them, like for instance, they way they seemed to always finish up looking so good a short time after they were almost destroyed. He couldn't bear to get rid of them and eventually they ended up buried underneath all the old timber and stuff in his shed. I remember when they were in the house, they were all shiny and looked like new. I seem to remember that we used to go on a short holiday at the same time every year. Dad never gave a reason for this but later on when I looked through his diaries, it was always during the anniversary of the bombing of the theatre."

Peter looked at his watch and stood up.

"Thank you very much Mr and Mrs Mills for all your help, and for giving up your afternoon to see us. I'm not sure if we did the right thing in finding out more about the seats. It's a little bit scary that your Dad actually experienced the same sort of phenomena as we have. At least nothing serious seems to have occurred, so perhaps it's all a bit of a coincidence. Anyway, thank you both once again for your help and we really enjoyed the tea and biscuits."

Mr and Mrs Mills shook hands with Peter and Betty, showed them to the door, and waved goodbye as they drove off.

They didn't say much on the way home and once there Betty set about preparing tea. Peter wandered into the lounge and looked thoughtfully at the theatre seats. The maroon upholstery was absolutely perfect, the wooden arms and backs were highly polished and the little brass numbers on the backs, numbers twenty five and twenty six, shone brightly.

When they had finished their meal and were clearing away the dishes, they talked about their visit to the Mills' that afternoon. Both of them were a little bit disturbed by what had evolved, but both were sensible people and now that a little bit if time had elapsed since their visit to Southport they were beginning to relax again although they both agreed that it was a little spooky. They had just sat down, Peter to read the evening paper, and Betty to do some sewing, when the telephone rang. Peter picked up the phone as he was nearest, and was surprised to find Mr Mills on the other end of the line.

"I'm so sorry to bother you Mr Matthews," he said, "my wife and I continued to look through Dad's diaries after you both left and we came up with a little more information. I don't know whether you will want to hear what we found out, as it is certainly a little strange."

Peter had a sudden feeling of déjà-vu. The short hairs on his neck prickled. He heard himself say, as if from a long way off, "Yes, of course we'd like to hear what you found out." His voice trembled a little.

Mr Mills said, "Well, if you're sure that you want to know, here it is. It turns out that the couple who were killed in the bombing, actually occupied seats twenty five and twenty six on the night they died. My wife's father found out this information sometime later and recorded it in his diary."

Peter felt a cold finger of fear touch his spine. He thanked Mr Mills for his phone call and put the receiver down, his hand shaking badly. He hesitantly related the information to Betty who tried valiantly not to show that the news had upset her. Peter was silent for a moment, his mind desperately trying to unravel the conundrum.

"Wasn't it Philip and Ethel Martin, they'd only been married two weeks?" Peter reached out and took Betty's hand.

"There's another coincidence love. Don't you see? They have the same initials as us. Philip and Ethel Martin, Peter and Betty Matthews."

"No," said Betty triumphantly, "we're P and B Matthews."

"Yes," said Peter, "Betty, short for Elizabeth, P and E Matthews," his voice rising as he realised the enormity of what he was saying.

"God, what a mess!" said Peter. "Where is all this leading? The day after tomorrow is the sixtieth anniversary of the raid. Do we ignore all this and carry on as usual? Do we get rid of those damn seats? I wish we'd never set eyes on them." He slumped down in the chair, his face ashen.

"I know," said Betty, "discretion being the better part of valour, why don't we do what Mrs Mills' father used to do on the anniversary. Let's have a weekend away. Let's go to our favourite place in the Lake District. Ring the hotel first thing in the morning and we'll set off immediately you get home from work on Friday afternoon." Her husband's face brightened perceptibly, he thought for a moment, then leaping to his feet, threw his arms around his wife and gave her a great hug.

"A brilliant idea, sweetheart, why didn't I think of that? Let's do it." On Friday morning Peter called the hotel in the Lake District, and as luck would have it, they had a vacancy.

Betty had a bag packed for them when he got home from work early in the afternoon. They had a quick snack then rushed around the bungalow locking windows and doors, not wanting to spend any longer there than absolutely necessary. Peter put their weekend bag in the car, and with hardly a backward glance, set off for the Lake District.

The weather that weekend was glorious. The lakes were absolutely beautiful in the bright sunshine. The pair of them relaxed as they strolled around Bowness and Windermere thinking to themselves that it really was a lovely place to visit. On Saturday night they had a wonderful meal and a few drinks, probably more than they should have, and retired to bed in a very happy and relaxed state of mind, the events of the past few days totally forgotten.

It was only as they neared home on Sunday afternoon that their minds returned to what might, or might not, be waiting for them. However they pushed these thoughts to the back of their minds and eventually Peter turned the car into the bottom of the road where they lived.

The sight that met their eyes caused Peter to brake sharply, the old Rover skidding to a shuddering halt with Betty, arms outstretched, bracing herself against the dashboard. The road ahead was full of police cars, fire engines and men in yellow dayglow jackets. Fire hoses ran all over the road like demented snakes. Flashing lights of all colours winked on and off. There seemed to be rubble strewn all over the road and water from burst pipes and hoses ran into the drains. A Police Constable approached as Peter wound down the window.

"I'm afraid you can't come down here sir, there's been a bit of an incident," said the Policeman.

"But we live down here," said Peter.

"What number would that be sir?" asked the P.C.

"Number 73," Peter replied.

"Bear with me a moment, please sir," said the Officer. He walked off a few yards and spoke into his radio. A minute later a Police Superintendent accompanied by a WPC approached them from the scene of the incident. Peter stepped out of the car, he felt sick. The Policeman, who had first stopped them, now approached again this time accompanied by the Officer and the WPC.

"Hello sir," he said, "I'm Superintendent Parker, I gather you live at number 73 on this road. Would that be correct sir?"

"Yes," said Peter, "That is correct Superintendent." His face white.

"And would you be Mr Matthews?" Peter nodded again. The Officer now looked at Betty.

"Is this Mrs Matthews?" Betty nodded without speaking.

He turned to Peter again and said,

"Have you been away, sir?"

"Yes," replied Peter, "we went off on Friday evening for a weekend in the Lake District. We're just on our way back. Look, what on earth is going on Superintendent?" said Peter frantically.

"You've both been very lucky," said Superintendent Parker. "I'm sorry to have to tell you both that your home has been totally destroyed by an explosion. It happened at about eleven o'clock last night."

Peter grabbed the car door to steady himself. "My God," he whispered, half to himself. Betty had burst into tears and was sobbing uncontrollably in her seat in the car. The officer caught the eye of the WPC and nodded towards Betty. She went immediately to Betty's side and tried to comfort her.

"Would you like to take a look at your bungalow Mr Matthews?" Peter took a deep breath and started off up the road in the direction of his and Betty's home, or at least what was left of it, the Superintendent falling into step beside him.

When they arrived at the shattered wreckage of number 73, firemen were still combing through the rubble. The Superintendent shouted to them to stop their work, and the Officer in Charge came over to join Peter and the Policeman.

"It's all right Harry," said the Superintendent, "The owners have turned up, there's no need to go looking for them any longer."

The fire officer looked relieved and relaxed visibly.

"What the hell happened?" Peter said, "what caused the explosion? Was anyone hurt?" The words came out in his panic, and he hadn't noticed that he had grabbed the police officer's arm in a vice-like grip, in his agitation. The Superintendent gently but firmly prised his fingers from their hold.

"It's all right Mr Matthews, no-one was hurt. A few people were blown out of bed and a little upset about being put out of their homes whilst we investigated the cause of the bang."

"Have you found the cause?" Peter asked, looking anxiously at Superintendent Parker. "Was it a bomb?"

The policeman looked sharply at Peter, "What makes you think it was a bomb?" he asked.

"What else could it be?" Peter asked sheepishly. "What else would cause an explosion like that?

"It was most certainly not a bomb, Mr Matthews," the Police Officer replied, "by the way sir, did you rush out on Friday afternoon on the way to the Lake district?"

"Yes we did," Peter said, "it's quite a drive, and we left almost immediately after I arrived home from work. We stopped only to have a quick snack as we wanted an early start."

"Then it seems," said the Superintendent, "according to the experts, that in your hurry to leave, a gas tap was left on. The gas accumulated in the building for almost twenty four hours. The windows and doors were all tightly closed and at approximately eleven o'clock on Saturday night the central heating kicked in, because the temperature had dropped quite a bit, and that, as they say, was that. The gas ignited as the boiler lit up, and this is the result. Your home, as you can see is completely destroyed. I'm afraid we were unable to save anything at all. Oh, I tell a lie. There was one item, or it might be two. A pair of old theatre seats were rescued. They look in impossibly good condition considering what they have been through."

Peter fainted.

.... of Heaven or Hell?

I stood within a marble hall, so large I could not see it all.
Great columns reaching out of sight, their tops hidden from the light.
A thronging mass of people there, wandering blindly everywhere.
Some who moaned as though in pain, others cried out again, again.
Some were calm and in control, others like a soul demented,
shrieked in torment at their plight.

I looked around me in my fear, to see someone I recognised quite near.
Who was this man who cowered so, brought death to millions long ago?
His turn now to meet his end, judgement now to send his soul to hell,
well past its time.
A great light lit the gloom around, a thundering voice did sound,
calling each and everyone to account,
for deeds of great and small amount, of cruelty and torture.
The rape of nations, years of plunder, so called great men who tore the world asunder
and all for what?
Those men whose love was for themselves alone.

The day of reckoning was here.

The names were called, and one by one they stood before the dazzling throne.

In front of Him. naked and alone.

To hear His verdict on their lives, to suffer cuts from a thousand knives, for what they'd done to others.

I stood there silent, wondering why, someone as inconsequential as I should mix with beasts so short of pity for their fellow man.

Was I as they were, or did they believe they were as innocent as I?

Do we all think we make the world a better place by deeds we carry out to grace our egos and our lives?

My name was called, my turn to stand before His throne. I almost fell, so great my fear of finding Hell and retribution.

The light was dazzling white, so white I could not see.

A lonely terror stricken soul before Thee.

As I lay there prostrate on the ground, I could not make the slightest sound.

And as I thought my life would end, I could not speak, I could not comprehend how short a

future stretched before me. A voice I recognised was heard.

"Wake up with Wogan," was the cry!

I sat up startled, awoken by my radio alarm, still in my bed, I am not dead!

It was all a dream, no need to worry, I should not have had that late night curry.

Francis Brown

The Hurdy Gurdy Man

"Mum! Mum! The Hurdy Gurdy Man is out in the street. Can I have sixpence to have a ride on the roundabout? Please Mum, can I? Everyone else will be having a go."

Mother as usual was busy with her housework, but the Hurdy Gurdy man was quite a regular if infrequent visitor to the streets around the town where I lived in Northern Ireland. In the days before television any form of entertainment for children was welcomed and although sixpences didn't grow on trees, no mother would have her child being the only one on the street not to have a ride on the roundabout.

"Just a moment child, can't you see that I'm doing the washing? Give me a minute to dry my hands." Mum went off to get her purse, with me jumping up and down impatiently. The purse was found and sixpence extracted and the two of us went together to the front door.

Across the street a crowd of my friends, and usually their mothers, were gathered around the horse drawn roundabout. The owner, even though it was a mild spring day, was dressed in a long brown overcoat, flat cap, brown corduroy trousers, black leather gaiters and hobnail boots. He was a scruffy looking individual, needing a shave and some people said, smelling of porter. However he was good with us children and enjoyed a bit of banter with our parents, especially with the younger mothers. Many of our parents, and some grandparents too, remembered having rides on this same roundabout when they were children. No-one had a clue as to what age he might be, but he seemed to have been around forever. He was well known around the town as a bit of a character. His old horse was well cared for, its coat shone, and when he stopped to set up his roundabout, or Hurdy Gurdy as it was known locally, the old horse would get a chance to have some oats from his nosebag and a drink of water.

The Hurdy Gurdy itself was fixed to a wooden base, with an old car axle and wheels, complete with tyre fittings underneath. It consisted of a revolving platform which had several galloping horses and about the same number of wooden cars complete with steering wheels. Many years ago these had been painted in bright vibrant colours, but as the years had passed, they had become faded, bleached by the sun and dulled by rain.

The roundabout was driven by a handle, turned by the proprietor. As it revolved, the horses and the cars went up and down, much to the delight of us children riding on them. The length and speed of the ride was determined by many factors. The time of day for example was important, whether or not he was tired and how many customers he'd had to propel on the Hurdy Gurdy. The weather too, played its part. If it was too warm or too cold and of course how many of us children were on the contraption at any one time and how many were still waiting. All of us of course wanted to be first on and the crush would resemble a rugby scrum, but the owner would diplomatically, without appearing to, select at random the ones who were well mannered and patient. His reasoning being, that the ones who were so desperate to get on would wait until the next ride, whilst the quiet ones, if they had to wait, might lose interest and move away. When the cars and horses were filled up with wide eyed, excited, chattering children, he would ask our parents and the rest of us children to stand back. Going to the centre of the roundabout, he began to turn the handle and to the delight of the passengers, the Hurdy Gurdy would begin to revolve, slowly at first and then more quickly. This was accompanied by the wheezing notes of the William Tell Overture, the tempo of which rose and fell as the revolutions of the ride varied. The children, myself included, shouted and screamed with glee, huge smiles on our faces and likewise on the faces of our doting parents. Not all the children were happy of course. There was, the Hurdy Gurdy man said, always one or two in each street, who would bawl their heads off from start to finish. My mother told me when I was older that he had said he could tell how children would turn out later in life by the way they behaved on the Hurdy Gurdy. The ones who cried and had to be taken off the ride, never really made much of life, but the best performers in the big world were the ones, who whilst frightened, stuck it out to the end. They, in his opinion, and he had years of experience and the opportunities to see his theories proven, turned out to be the cream.

When the ride was over and everyone was satisfied, the Hurdy Gurdy man would head off to the next street in search of new customers and the whole sequence would begin again. We children who had enjoyed ourselves would sleep well that night and many of us would remember the Hurdy Gurdy man for the rest of our lives.

Several times in later years, whilst walking through the crowded market square, my eye would be taken by a gentleman leaning against a lamp post. Dressed in a long brown overcoat, flat cap, brown corduroy trousers, leather gaiters and hobnail boots, his dark brown eyes seemed to bore into mine and I'd try to look away, embarrassed, but not before he gives me a wink and a knowing smile. I'd look back a second later and there would be no-one there, and I would know that I had just seen the Hurdy Gurdy man, again.

Time Share

I want to tell you a story, as someone famous once said. You may or may not find it interesting but it might just make you think!

My name is Fred by the way, and my wife Jean and I decided to have a week's holiday in the sun, a last minute decision you understand. However the dates that we had chosen in February coincided with school half term holidays and so we found ourselves struggling to find last minute vacancies on package holidays. Any vacancies that we found were expensive to say the least. Even on the web sites there was nothing that we either fancied or could afford.

Then our local evening paper arrived and we had a look through the adverts. Have you ever had the feeling that some things are meant to happen? Well it didn't cross our minds at the time, but it certainly did later on. There in the column headed 'Holidays' was a three line advert for a small private hotel in Tenerife. All inclusive at what was to us, a particularly low price. A telephone number completed the advert.

We were getting quite desperate by now as we were only a few days away from being on holiday with nowhere to go, I decided to ring the number. The phone was answered on the second ring by a gentleman, who spoke English with a faint Spanish accent, and introduced himself as the manager. I explained about the advert and he confirmed that the price quoted was correct, and that they had one double en suite room free if Mr. and Mrs. Smyth would like to book. I said that we would first of all need to check on the availability of a flight to Tenerife. He would, he said, hold our booking for twenty four hours and we could ring him back with the details and we were not to worry about getting to and from the airport as transport would be arranged no matter what time of day or night we arrived. I promised to ring him back as soon as possible and broke the connection.

Two things registered in my mind at the time. One, the manager had answered the phone in English, how did he know that the caller was English? Two, he had asked if Mr. and Mrs. Smyth would like to book. I could not remember telling him my name, so how did he know that? However, in the excitement of the possibility of our holiday plans being resurrected, these questions faded into insignificance and next morning first thing I contacted our local travel agent and enquired about flights to and from Tenerife, not really expecting any joy on that front. To our surprise there were seats available. The outward flight leaving at eight thirty am and the return at six o'clock in the morning from Tenerife, which would mean an early start from the hotel on the way home, probably about three o'clock in the morning. We booked the flights and excitedly rang the hotel again. The phone was answered by the same gentleman as before.

"Ah Senor Smyth, you and your lovely wife are coming to stay with us are you not?"

"How did you know that?" I asked.

"Sometimes I have a feeling about these things Senor Smyth," he said. "You are coming to stay with us?"

"Yes we are Mister…..?

"I am so sorry Senor Smyth I am being very rude, my name is Estofan, or in English, Steven and I am the hotel manager, now when will you be joining us?"

I gave him the details of the flight and he assured me that the arrival and the early departure at the end of our stay would be no problem at all. He explained that the hotel, the Marietta, though small with fifteen bedrooms, was quite exclusive. He likened it to being like a club, the guests being the members who came back time after time. It was only when someone was unable to return for one reason or another that a vacancy came up, as had happened on this occasion. The hotel, he said was a little off the beaten track in the north of the island, close to Puerto de la Cruz, and situated on the slopes of Mount Teide. Jean and I had been to Tenerife once before some years ago, and so we remembered that this was quite a nice area. The manager also suggested that as it was so close to our holiday date that we could pay by cheque when we arrived at the hotel. I thought that this was a little odd as most places of business these days would just ask for a debit card or credit card number. He explained that the Hotel Marietta was a little old fashioned in that respect and stressed that a cheque on arrival would be adequate. He finished by saying that he and his staff were looking forward to seeing us and promised us a holiday to remember.

Jean and I were over the moon. We had booked our holiday in the sun at a super price and we would be off in a few days. We couldn't wait.

Our flight landed at the airport in the south of the island and, once our passports had been checked, we collected our luggage from the conveyor and made our way out of the arrivals lounge to the car park. Neither of us mentioned it at the time but we were both a little concerned that perhaps no one would turn up to meet us. However all was well. As we left the main building, a man wearing a chauffeur's uniform, complete with peaked cap and gleaming black knee high boots, carrying a card with Mr. and Mrs. Smyth written on it, stepped forward and introduced himself as Miguel, our driver for the two hour trip north to the Hotel Marietta.

He took our bags and led us to an absolutely beautiful vintage Rolls Royce, which being a car buff I guessed was a 1934 Continental Phantom drop head coupe. Miguel opened the passenger side door and Jean and I slid into the soft leather rear seat. He deposited our bags in the large trunk on the back of the car climbed into the driver's seat started up the engine and moved smoothly out of the car park and onto the highway north. As it was a fine day the top was down on the old car, but despite the fact that the speedometer hovered around ninety to one hundred kilometres an hour, there was virtually no wind noise at all in the back and so we relaxed in comfort to enjoy the first stage of our holiday.

Just over an hour later we turned off the main trunk road having by-passed Santa Cruz, the capital, and took the road to La Oratava. We began to climb steadily as we reached the foothills of Mount Teide, the road narrowing and beginning to twist and turn. Other traffic was non existent. As we reached the tree line, mostly pine and fir, the sun, which had been shining warmly all the way from the airport, was replaced by cloud and mist. Miguel stopped the car in a lay by and quickly and expertly put up the hood whilst apologising all the while for the change in the weather. The old car moved off again, climbing effortlessly up the ever steeper gradient the mist turning to rain, not a downpour but the windscreen wipers were working hard. About twenty minutes later the sun began to break through again between the thinning trees. A short time later the car slowed and turned off the roadway between two granite gateposts and onto a wide driveway, which cut a swathe through the trees, before arriving in front of an imposing nineteenth century, three storied building. We drove beneath a sandstone archway into a courtyard and stopped by a curved, gently rising walkway leading up to a pair of open, arched wooden doors.

The limousine had barely come to rest before a smiling gentleman dressed in a black jacket, dazzlingly white shirt, grey tie, pinstripe trousers and highly polished shoes, walked smartly down to the car, accompanied by a bellboy who opened the door. We climbed out and the man, whom we had rightly assumed to be the hotel manager, shook us both warmly by the hand.

"Welcome to the Hotel Marietta, Senora et Senor Smyth. I hope that you have enjoyed your journey from the airport and that our Miguel has been looking after you well. I am the hotel manager, my name, as I think I told you when we spoke on the telephone, is Estofan or in English, Steven. As I feel that we are old friends already, please feel free to call me Steven. My staff and I will do everything possible to make your stay with us a happy and memorable one."

"Paco, please take Senor and Senora Smyth's luggage to their room while I complete the formalities of checking in so that their holiday can begin."

The manager led us up to the hotel entrance and into the reception area where he went behind a polished counter and produced a thick ledger which he turned towards us and asked us to sign our full names and address. Both of us noticed that we were the only entries on that page. He then scanned our passports briefly and handed them back to us with a little smile. I had a cheque ready to hand over on arrival and he smiled again, nodding graciously as he accepted it before placing it in the safe without even a glance at it.

Several couples were sitting around on the comfortable chairs and sofas in the lounge area just beyond the entrance hall. It was now late afternoon and most of them were drinking cocktails served by a waiter working from a bar in the corner of the room.

"Dinner," he said, "will be served in the dining room from eight thirty onwards." The manager then beckoned for the bellboy to show us to our room and again wished us a pleasant stay at the Hotel Marietta.

Our room, en suite, was spacious and well appointed. A large window opened out onto a balcony which overlooked the forest and lower slopes of Mount Teide. Just visible in the distance, was the town of Puerto de la Cruz and the sea. After we had put our holiday clothing away in the large wardrobes, we relaxed for a few minutes prior to going down to dinner. It was then that I noticed that unlike other hotels that we had stayed in on previous holidays abroad, there was no television in our room. We presumed that perhaps we had to hire one from reception. Using the phone, one of those old Bakelite ones, on our bedside table, I rang reception. The young lady, who answered in very good English, seemed a little surprised at our request, and explained apologetically, that televisions were not supplied by the hotel. I thanked her and decided that a TV was not really necessary anyway.

Our first visit to the dining room for our evening meal was pleasantly surprising. There was a table with our room number on it, number thirteen, (we are not superstitious), reserved for us. We had become used to the system used by package holiday hotels of serve yourself buffet meals, but the Hotel Marietta had waiter service from the kitchen to the table. The food was superb, cooked to absolute perfection. The wines were excellent and always at the correct temperature.

There were fifteen tables, one for each of the hotel rooms and most had middle aged couples sitting at them. One had two elderly ladies sharing and one with an elderly gentleman on his own.

Most of the ladies were in long skirts and blouses, whilst the gentlemen wore slacks with shirt and tie. There was a distinct absence of the usual holiday wear of tee shirts, shorts and sandals. It was a little more formal than that without being too stuffy. There was a small dance floor about five metres square in front of a stage where later in the evening a trio of Spanish musicians played a selection of instruments and entertained the guests. The other thing that we noticed was that smoking was allowed in the dining room, although only a small number of people did and they were seated in a special area.

The general feel of the place was that it was faintly reminiscent of the sixties and seventies, and we, being on the wrong side of fifty, thoroughly enjoyed it.

Next day we enquired at reception about the bus service to Puerto de la Cruz. The young lady on duty quickly called Miguel the chauffeur and he brought the Rolls to the front door. He drove us into Puerto de la Cruz, and asked us what time we would like to be picked up for our return to the hotel. The car and himself were at the disposal of the guests and was part of the service, although, he hastened to add, few if any ever made use of it. Most of them, he explained liked to sit around the small swimming pool or walk in the very extensive grounds of the hotel. We took up the offer several times during our week and Miguel seemed happy to show us around the island.

We talked to a few of the guests and they were very nice people, most of them from various parts of the UK. They seemed reserved, not stand offish or anything like that, but there was something that I could not quite put my finger on. I had brought along my new digital camera and had taken pictures of some of the other guests, usually after we had had a drink or two, and they had mellowed a little. They were quite taken by the camera especially when we were able to show them their pictures on the small screen at the back. They seemed to find the technology very amusing.

Our week's holiday absolutely flew in and it seemed like no time at all before it was time to go home. We said our goodbyes to our fellow guests and of course to Steven the hotel manager, who enquired if we had enjoyed our stay and hoped that we would return, like many of the other guests. We replied that we had and we would.

We set off from the hotel on our journey to the airport at about two am, driven by Miguel in the Rolls, our flight being at six am and of course we had to check in two hours before. We thanked Miguel profusely and offered him a sizeable tip which he refused, saying that he was only doing his job which he loved, and that he was looking forward to seeing us again in the near future.

And so we returned home again and went back to work feeling refreshed and invigorated and looking forward to our next vacation.

We had been home about a week when we met an old friend whom we hadn't seen for some time. He noticed our suntan enquiring if we had been away on holiday. We told him about Tenerife and the Hotel Marietta. He seemed a little surprised and said that it must have reopened again. He had stayed there with his wife some years ago, when Tenerife was still in the throes of opening up to the tourist trade. He said that shortly after he had stayed there in the late sixties, he remembered reading in the national press about the hotel being destroyed by fire and that there had been great loss of life. He suggested that if we were interested that our local library might have something in its archives about it.

We thought no more about it and in the next few days, I decided to put our holiday pictures onto our computer intending to print a few off. When I started to view the pictures on the screen some of the pictures were excellent, but the ones that we had taken of the guests and ourselves now only had us on them. We had not one picture of anyone other than ourselves and yet we had viewed the pictures at the hotel and they had been fine. I decided that there had to be a problem with the camera. We took it to the shop where we had bought it, but despite every test that they did, it was working perfectly.

A little nagging doubt began to form in my mind and we went, purely out of curiosity, to the City Library. There I gave the librarian the approximate date of the supposed disaster at the Hotel Marietta in Tenerife saying that it had been reported in the national press at the time. Modern technology has meant that the contents of newspapers can be stored on a microdot. After trawling through dozens of these, suddenly there it was! February 1966. The text told of the small highly rated Hotel Marietta Hotel in Tenerife being totally destroyed by fire in the early hours of the morning. The fire had spread so quickly that none of the guests in the building, most of them elderly, had escaped the blaze. Twenty seven people holidaying there and four staff including the Manager, Senor Estofan Pedrilla had perished in the conflagration.

The only survivors were the chauffeur, Senor Miguel Lopez, and an English couple, Mr. and Mrs. Smyth whom he had driven to the airport at two o'clock in the morning, apparently just a short time before the hotel was engulfed in flames.

By the way our cheque was never cashed.

Ad Infinitum

In the Spring I thought I saw you several times. A sighting from afar. A hair style, colouring, a profile glimpsed in a crowded room. But none of them were you. You were a germ of an ancient memory revived and recognised when I saw someone with similar looks, wherever I might be. But none of them were you.

Spring turns to Summer and over many years I never had a sighting to raise my hopes. I turned along another path. A path I would not have taken had I found you, but a path I stuck to and persevered with, until in late Summer I arrived at a place I had never visited before.

In a room full of so many people my memory was suddenly jolted when I saw you before me. I knew without a doubt that it was you, and subsequently that you had known me. All this happened as I began to fear that our renewal would perhaps miss out on a generation or two.

Our finding each other was like a melting pot of pure emotion. We were together again.

And now in Autumn we are once again on the same path. A path bordered by many flowers, that we have walked before, many times, in peace, love and harmony.

We must remember when Winter comes, that whilst we may be separated, then without a doubt we will walk that very same path again. It is decreed ad infinitum.

Francis Brown

Jennifer

Jennifer walked slowly into the dining room. It was just after eight o'clock on a wintry Tuesday morning in February. Her mother and father were just finishing off their coffee and buttered toast before dashing off to work. Neither of her parents were morning people and they didn't pay her any attention whatsoever as she sat down at the other end of the long dining table. She thought that they seemed more preoccupied than usual this morning, but she sat quietly and said nothing to interrupt their mood.

Her father eventually tossed the morning paper onto the dining table and left the dining room to get his raincoat and briefcase. Her mum tidied the breakfast table and without speaking, went upstairs to get ready to go to work. Jennifer, who really didn't feel like any breakfast this morning, had sat watching her parents, thinking how much older they looked. She had been away for a little while and now she had returned to her own home again. Her father was a sales manager for a credit company, whilst her mum ran her own beauty salon. They both worked similar hours and as their businesses were both literally in the same street, they tended to travel together in the family car.

She spoke to them several times as they rushed about preparing to set off for the day, but they were so engrossed with their own thoughts that they didn't hear her. Jennifer was beginning to think that she had done something awful to annoy them and felt uncomfortable in the silence, so it was a relief when they eventually went off and left her to her own devices.

As she stood up from her seat at the end of the dining table, Jennifer noticed idly that the morning paper was opened at the obituary column. The reason for her parent's preoccupation at breakfast became clear. Obviously someone they knew, possibly a colleague, had passed away, and she felt a little bit better in the knowledge that she had not been responsible for their sombre mood.

She wandered into the living room, the picture of her in her graduation cap and gown with her proud parents on either side still had place of honour on the mantelpiece. Those were the days, first class honours in Theology. She walked around her home, touching things that brought back so many happy memories. She went upstairs and as usual the doors to the three bedrooms were open. She went first into her parent's room, the bed made up as always by her mother, and the room tidied before she left. 'You never know,' she had said, 'who might come to visit.' Jennifer smiled at the memory. The spare bedroom was also neat and tidy, the bed made up and ready.

At last she went into her own room. It looked as it had the last time that she had seen it twelve months before. The same matching duvet cover and pillow cases, the pastel pink curtains, her dressing table still with her perfumes neatly set out, a hint of her favourite one still hanging in the air. The wardrobe door was ajar and she saw that all her clothing was still in there. It was nice to be home again, even if her parents were too engrossed with other things to speak to her this morning. She was sure that all would be well when they got home this evening. She lay down on her bed and slept.

She awoke to the sound of voices downstairs and looked at the illuminated dial of her bedside clock. It was almost seven o'clock and her room was in darkness. She realised that the voices belonged to her parents, who had obviously just come home from work. She leapt off the bed and raced downstairs into the living room. Her parents looked up, startled by the commotion as she ran to them, hugging and kissing them in turn. Her mother burst into tears of happiness as she embraced her daughter.

"Jennifer, why didn't you let us know that you were coming? Oh it's so wonderful to see you."

Her dad hugged both of them and steered them both into the living room and they sat down on the large settee, all of them overcome with the joy of being together again. What a change from this morning, Jennifer thought.

They were so engrossed with their reunion that no one heard the letter box rattle as the local evening paper arrived and dropped, front page open, onto the hall carpet.

The headline read:

LOCAL BUSINESS COUPLE DIE IN
HORROR SMASH WITH SNOWPLOUGH.

The article went on to recount the death of their daughter in a similar accident, exactly one year before.

Just a Minute.

"What time is it?" the old man said,
"Time to get up, or time for bed?
I never know what day it is,
I go by what the young nurse says."

They wash me, feed me, even wipe my nose,
They comb my hair and put on my clothes.
I'm grateful for each thing they do.
They work so hard, they are so few.

They've got to rush off, perhaps next door,
They've just found someone on the floor.
I'm left alone lying on my bed,
"We won't be long," the nurse had said.

It's not easy to move to a Nursing Home
But my family had said it was the right place to come.
"You'll be well looked after, night and day."
That's very easy for them to say.

The staff are few, the patients wearing,
It must be hard to be so caring
When the pressure's on and there's lots to do,
To take the time for a word or two.

I used to be a leader of men,
I don't suppose I'll be that again.
I treated everyone the same
And took the time to learn their name.

Civility doesn't cost so much
A smile, a joke, a friendly touch.
To be treated with dignity by all
Can make a lonely soul stand tall.

And so you staff with lots to do
The people you help think a lot of you.
Take a minute from your labours,
It'll make our day and brighten yours.

Francis Brown

The Garret

A few months ago I had occasion to visit the town where I was born, more than sixty years ago. It was early on a Sunday morning and I was driving past the row of old terraced houses, once the homes of the families of men who worked in the local gas works. The obsolete coal gas plant had been demolished to make room for a modern housing development. Now apparently it was to be the turn of the row of eight houses to suffer the same fate, all in the name of progress of course. The first house in the row also contained a corner shop, where my grandparents had lived. Grandmother looked after the shop and my grandfather had a grocery round. He had an old cart pulled by a well fed, well looked after pony, working around the streets of the town carrying everything from fruit and vegetables to bottles of pop and confectionery for his customers.

I was born upstairs in the house next door, in the larger of the two bedrooms, on a cold November day in 1942. It took a combined team of a doctor, the local midwife and, of course, my mother to get me into this world. A forceps delivery I learned when I was older.

I remembered these things as I drove slowly past my old home, now looking run down and dilapidated. It had been empty for some time, as had the rest of the houses in the row. On a sudden impulse I turned the car around and drove back to my grandparent's house, where there was a bit of waste ground. My grandfather had a gateway into the yard at the back of the house where he stabled the pony. I had been in there many, many times and I checked to see if the gate had been locked. To my surprise I found that it wasn't and I managed to squeeze in past a large JCB digger and other items of demolition equipment. Obviously, the demise of the row was only a short step away. The old stable which had backed onto an adjoining wall of my house had been demolished or had fallen down, so I climbed onto the cab of the digger and looked over the wall into the backyard of my old home. The walls had been built of sandstone, rough plastered then whitewashed. Over the years the once smooth surface had crumbled, corroded away by the elements.

I decided on the spur of the moment that I was going to take a look in the house for one last time before it disappeared for ever. Luckily I wasn't going anywhere in a hurry, nor was I wearing my best bib and tucker, so I hoisted myself on top of the wall and dropped into the back yard. I tiptoed up to the old kitchen door which hung on only one hinge. I have no idea why I tiptoed to the door, only perhaps because I felt a little bit guilty about trespassing, but anyway there was no-one to see me. I pushed the old door open, its hinges broken and twisted, and went inside. The house had been empty for some years and the smell of damp and decay was noticeable. The kitchen area was empty except for some of the workman's tools that were stored there. The living room was dark even in daylight, just as it had always been, although I could have found my way round it blindfolded if I needed to. Some of the panes of glass in the small windows had been broken, allowing the rain and anything else to come in. I crunched through broken glass and heaven knows what else as I wandered through the downstairs room with its peeling wallpaper. The wall between the front room and the living room had been removed years before in an attempt to allow more light into the living area. The front door was securely locked and barred. I turned my attention to the upstairs of the old house. The stairs still had scraps of the old lino tacked to them and they creaked ominously as I ascended slowly to the landing. Straight ahead was my parent's bedroom, its door askew, the one where I had first seen the light of day sixty years ago. I went inside, once more crunching on broken glass.

Memories came flooding back as I stood there, the old cast iron fireplace on the wall to the right, the wartime utility wardrobe on the left. My parent's double bed would have been immediately on my right, parallel with the front wall of the house with its two windows. I remember these same windows having blackout curtains pulled over them during the war. Another memory came to mind of my father getting a job in the gasworks and he needed an alarm clock to wake him up in the morning for his shift. He had to apply for a permit to purchase one, I presume because it could have been used to set off an explosive device, and our Prudential insurance man gave him a character reference. Years later the old clock was still giving sterling service.

I went over to the front windows and looked out across the street to the back gateway of Wallace's public house. Many times as a lad, I would with some of my friends, watch the draymen drop the huge barrels of porter off the side of their wagon onto hessian bags filled with corks. We would then roll the barrels up the yard to the back door of the pub, and when the job was done the draymen would perhaps give us tuppence each for some sweets from my Grandmother's shop.

I dragged myself from my reverie and entered my own room at the bottom of the attic stairs. There was nothing in there at all, just memories. I walked to the window and looked out over the back yard and the kitchen roof. I could also see the old gasworks yard, now built upon. I shut my eyes and imagined that I could hear the thump of the exhaust from the steam pump as it raised water from an underground well to feed the Lancashire boilers. I turned and left and almost went back downstairs. Then the garret beckoned.

I stood looking up into the gloom of the old attic, remembering the floor boards with dry rot. The only window was an old skylight in the roof, and it was always in a state of semi darkness as there was no electric light up there. However, it was probably my favourite place in the whole house. That's where all the treasures were. There were pieces of old Victorian pottery, large earthenware jugs and matching bowls, decorated with flowers. Old black and white framed prints and suitcases with all sorts of junk in, the sort of junk that you see these days on *The Antiques Road Show*. There were cartons of hundreds, if not thousands of brown buttons of varying sizes, and hundreds of grease nipples. A huge flag pole, perhaps three inches in diameter and eight or nine feet long, complete with a union flag. To be flown where? I have no idea. There were boxes containing all sorts of bits and bobs. I remember finding a small pistol which excited me greatly. It seemed quite old and not a toy. Part of the handle was missing and it was probably a point 22 calibre and pretty well rusted up. When you are seven or eight years old, to find something like that was exciting! My mother was forever telling me not to go up there, but she was at work all day and so when I got home from school, I could do as I liked. It was, as I say, my favourite place in the house, a place of mystery and imagination. Now I just had to go up there one more time.

I climbed the dusty stairs slowly, wishing that I had a torch so that I could see better. I reached the top of the stairs safely even though the banister was missing and looked around in the little bit of light that the cracked skylight let in. The furthest recesses at the bottom of the roof timbers were in almost complete darkness. The wooden boards creaked as I stepped on them and spotting an old wooden chair in the centre of the floor, I carefully made my way over to it. I picked up an old rag, wiped the dust from the seat and sat down to reflect for a moment in the gloom, my memory and imagination working overtime.

Everything in the old attic was as I remembered it. Everything!

I don't know how long I sat there, lost in my childhood. I slowly became aware of something or someone watching me. I couldn't see anything at first but I slowly began to make out a faint outline in the half light. I felt a chill come over me, goose bumps on my arms and the hair on my neck rising. I desperately resisted the urge to flee. The figure became a little clearer until I was able to make out the outline of a young boy. He was dressed in grey shirt, grey short trousers down past his knees and a sleeveless fair-isle jumper. On his feet he wore grey knee length socks and brown leather sandals. His fair hair was cut in a fringe and he looked vaguely familiar. I guessed his age to be eight or nine years old. He was sitting on an old suitcase and was watching me intently.

"Who are you and what are you doing here?" I managed to say, my voice a little louder than usual. He just sat and watched me. Silent!

Again I asked, "Who are you?"

He looked at me questioningly, "Don't you know?" His voice was young yet strong.

I was gradually beginning to get over my initial fright and it was being replaced by annoyance at this youngster.

"No I don't know," I said, my voice a little more firm. "Are you going to tell me or what?"

"In a moment," he said. He put his head a little on one side and studied me closely for a minute. "I know who you are."

"Okay then, who am I?"

"You are me. I am you as you were at my age. You are what I should have grown to be. When you left this house you left me and your youth, behind you. I never knew whether I lived or died, whether I married and became a father. My fear of growing old outweighed my fear of not growing old. Now I know how my life turned out."

I was totally speechless, my mind in turmoil. I wanted to flee from this nightmare. I sat there immobile as the lad walked across to me. We seemed to blend into each other. Suddenly all was dark for a moment and when I opened my eyes I was sitting on an old suitcase, watching myself walking purposefully down the stairs from the garret.

Cat Flap

My friend Arthur was telling me recently that he and his wife Betty were shopping one Saturday afternoon in a little town in the Lake District. They came upon one of those very twee little shops, you know the ones, they sell crystal glasses, Royal Doulton ornaments, kitchen tools, hand painted place mats and all things expensive and deemed necessary for the perfect kitchen in every home. He really didn't know why they went inside at all, other than the fact that it was a freezing cold day and the rain had just come on. It was nice and warm in the shop and they strolled around, along with other people, sheltering from the rain and looking at all the lovely things they didn't need and couldn't afford even if they did.

Arthur and his wife wandered into an alcove, which appeared to be the area where the items which had not sold well were offered at reduced prices. It was here that they found 'Kat', or rather he found them. As they walked around this sale area, Arthur managed to trip over something which had been left on the floor. He just managed to stop himself from knocking over a stack of crystal glassware which, even though they were seconds, would have cost him a pretty penny to replace. He glared down at the offending obstacle, and there he was, Kat.

Kat was about fifteen inches high, jet black in colour, and fat with it. His head tilted back so that he appeared to be looking upwards at anyone standing in front of him, or it! He, Betty and Arthur assumed it was a 'he', had the most amazing pair of large emerald green eyes, which, no matter where you stood in front of him, seemed to be looking at you. They quickly realised that Kat, as they came to christen him, was in fact a doorstop and Betty and Arthur were quite taken with him, as they were fond of cats anyway. To cut a long story short, his price had been slashed to just under half of what it had been and even though they didn't actually need a cat shaped doorstop, they finished up taking one home with them.

Kat duly took up residence in Arthur and Betty's semi and all was well for some time. He stood guard at most of the downstairs rooms, holding doors open as required, and all was right with the world. Friends and neighbours would call from time to time and most of them would remark on the new doorstop and especially his lifelike green eyes that seemed to follow them round the house. Gradually Arthur and Betty became so used to Kat that he just merged into the background and they hardly noticed him any longer.

One day Betty had gone out to the shops and Arthur had gone upstairs to the spare bedroom to look for something or other, and, as he went through the door he tripped and almost fell over something on the floor. It was Kat his big green eyes looked up sheepishly at Arthur, who only just refrained from drop kicking him out of sight. Instead he put him on the bed and made a mental note to have a word with Betty about where she placed him in future. The weather had become warmer with the coming of early summer and doors in the house were left open, so Kat came into his own, holding them open to let fresh air into the house. Then one day their next door neighbour arrived in a very agitated state, claiming that her pet toy poodle had shot into her house at a high rate of knots, absolutely terrified and trembling all over. She had rushed into the garden and claimed she had seen a large black animal disappear through the hedge into Arthur's garden. Arthur, Betty and their neighbour searched the gardens but nothing was found. There were no more reports of anything out of the ordinary and all returned to normality.

A few days later Arthur was sitting in his favourite chair reading the sports page of his newspaper, when Betty came back from the shops. Usually she would regale Arthur about the bargains she had found and gossip she had heard while she had been out, but this day, nothing. Not a word. Arthur went through to the kitchen where Betty was putting the groceries away and he saw immediately that she was not in a good mood. Men have a sixth sense about these things. After a couple of minutes of the silent treatment he gave in.

"Okay, what have I done now?" he asked.

"You mean you don't know?" Betty replied caustically.

"No, what have I done that's so terrible?" Arthur asked.

"You could have got me killed by doing something as stupid as that."

"What on earth are you on about? I haven't done anything, Betty."

"You put that blooming cat on the back seat of the car. I had to do an emergency stop and the damn thing hit me on the back of the head and scared the life out of me. I'm still shaking now." Betty rarely swore so Arthur knew that things were indeed serious.

"I meant to say to you," she continued," about moving it around the house. I keep finding it all over the place. I bet you used it to scare next door's dog as well, you never did like the little brute."

"Funny you should say that, Betty, but I was going to say the same thing to you. I've found it in some strange places in the house as well and I thought you had moved it. Where is it now then?"

"It's still in the back of the car, outside the garage."

"Right," said Arthur, "let's have a look." They went out to the car and there, sure enough, on the floor in the back lay Kat. Arthur picked him up walked up to the garden shed, opened the door and unceremoniously tossed Kat in, not noticing as he did so that the big green eyes had a slightly troubled look. He locked the door and took the key indoors, hanging it on the key board in the kitchen. Arthur and Betty kissed and made up, although neither of them was fully satisfied that the other was not playing tricks on them. However they both saw the funny side of things and neither could remain angry with the other for long and so things returned to normal.

After a couple of weeks Kat was still out in the shed, out of sight out of mind as they say. Arthur and Betty went out one Saturday night to have dinner with some friends, and as they arrived back home at about midnight, they found a police car, blue lights flashing, outside their house. As they pulled up an ambulance arrived as well. They got out of the car and were met by a Police Officer accompanied by their next door neighbour, who explained that they had heard noises coming from their house and knowing that there was no-one in, (Betty always asked them to keep an eye on things when she and Arthur were out late), rang the Police. On arriving, the Police Officer had discovered that the back door had been forced and on entering had found a burglar lying injured at the bottom of the stairs looking like he had suffered a broken leg. The ambulance people were now dealing with him. Later as they carried him off to the ambulance he was muttering something about tripping over a cat at the top of the stairs.

When Arthur and Betty were eventually allowed to go into their house, after the police had finished taking fingerprints et cetera, they went to the bottom of the stairs and looked up to the landing, and, saw sitting there looking down at them, his big green eyes twinkling as if to say "Forgive me?" was Kat.

Lightning Source UK Ltd.
Milton Keynes UK
25 July 2010

157417UK00002B/2/P

9 781452 008097